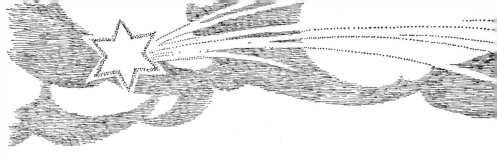

The Hunting of

Illustrated by Alexy Pendle

the Unicorn

Carol James

ANDRE DEUTSCH

Books by the same author

ANNA AND THE MINI-MAN

First published 1973 by
André Deutsch Limited
105 Great Russell Street London WC1

Copyright © 1973 by Carol James
All rights reserved

Printed in Great Britain by
Ebenezer Baylis & Son Ltd
The Trinity Press Worcester and London

ISBN 0 233 96402 9

FOR EMMA AND CLAIRE RIDLEY
WITH LOVE

Contents

♣

CHAPTER I

Paul-Paul Dupont

♣

PAUL-PAUL DUPONT was French. His name was not really Paul-Paul – it was just plain Paul. But everyone had always called him Paul-Paul.

Paul-Paul lived in a village at the edge of a big forest, not very far from Paris, which is the capital city of France. The village was called Fleury-des-Bois, and Paul-Paul's father was the village postman.

But Paul-Paul hardly knew Fleury-des-Bois at all. He had been ill in bed for a very long time. He was so ill that he wasn't even allowed to sit up. All he could do was lie and look out of his bedroom window at the sky, and listen to the other children playing outside. He could hardly remember what the village looked like, or what it was like to play with other children.

Being ill for such a long time had made Paul-Paul very small for his age. He also had dark curly hair, and a round face, with a nose like a little beak. And he had big, round, dark eyes with sleepy eyelids, which he blinked a great deal. Altogether, he looked very like an owl, especially when he was daydreaming, which was most of the time. There wasn't much else to do.

Paul-Paul often daydreamed about the big forest next to the village. His house was the last house in the village before the forest started, so that its trees were very close to his window. During the day, he could hear the leaves rustling and the birds singing, and at night he could hear the owls hooting, and the foxes yapping and howling far, far away in the wildest depths of the forest. It sounded just like a fairy-tale forest to Paul-Paul. He liked to imagine how he would go for long walks there when he was well again, and all the strange wild animals he would see.

Paul-Paul had never been for a really long walk in the forest, not even before he was ill, because he had been too young then. He had never seen any real wild rabbits or squirrels or foxes. This made it very difficult for him to imagine what it was like in the forest. He wished someone would tell him stories about it, so that he could imagine it better. He especially wished someone would tell him fairy-tales about magic forests in the olden days, and the adventures people had had there, so that he could imagine having adventures like that himself.

Paul-Paul had quite a large family, but they were all very busy most of the time. His mother and grandmother were very busy with the cooking and shopping and housework, and his father was very busy delivering letters and parcels. Paul-Paul also had a brother and a sister, but they were much older than he was. They were already grown up. His sister, Rose-Marie, who was very pretty, was busy working at the hairdresser's in the village square all day; and his brother, Louis-Philippe, was away in the Army, and hardly ever came home on leave.

So poor Paul-Paul was alone nearly all the time, lying in bed and looking out of his window at the sky, and trying to make up stories about the forest and the olden days all by himself.

One day, just when Paul-Paul was feeling so sad, and bored, and lonely that he could hardly bear it any longer, his mother opened his bedroom door, and said, 'Here's a special visitor to see you, Paul-Paul.' And into Paul-Paul's room came a very pretty girl, even prettier than Rose-Marie, and about the same age as she was. She was so pretty, with her long fair hair, and her smiling grey eyes, and her lovely blue dress, with a blue ribbon in her hair to match it, that Paul-Paul could hardly believe that she wasn't a fairy-tale princess.

'This is your cousin, Marie-Céleste Dubois,' said Paul-Paul's mother. 'She's been away at college in Paris for such a long time, I don't suppose you remember her. But here she is, home on holiday – and as soon as she heard you were ill in bed, she came round to see you.'

Paul-Paul's mother went away, and Marie-Céleste sat down on

the edge of Paul-Paul's bed. First of all, she took a little ginger-bread man out of her basket and gave it to Paul-Paul, and then she said, 'Now then! What do you like best – talking, or guessing-games, or stories?'

'Stories!' said Paul-Paul.

'What sort of stories?' asked Marie-Céleste.

'Fairy-tales,' said Paul-Paul, 'about the olden days, and the forest.'

'That's lucky,' said Marie-Céleste. 'That's my favourite sort of story too, so I know lots of them.' And she settled herself more comfortably on the edge of Paul-Paul's bed, and began, 'Once upon a time, long, long ago, there was a big, wild, magic forest . . .'

Paul-Paul lay back on his pillows, eating his gingerbread man, and listening happily. The story was lovely and long, and full of all the things he had always wanted to hear about – enchanted castles, and princes and princesses, and knights, and dragons, and unicorns. Marie-Céleste was so good at story-telling, Paul-Paul could almost believe that the story was really happening. It was just as if he was back in the olden days himself, and his little room seemed to be full of the galloping of hoofs, and the flashing of swords, and the roaring of terrible dragons.

'My goodness, what rosy cheeks you've got now!' said Paul-Paul's mother, coming in with his tea just as the story was finished. And it was true that Paul-Paul felt better than he had for a long time. He was tingling all over with excitement from the story.

'I'll come back tomorrow,' promised Marie-Céleste, 'and tell you another one.'

Sure enough, back she came the next afternoon, and every afternoon after that for the rest of her holiday. Every day she brought Paul-Paul a gingerbread man from the baker's shop in the village square, which belonged to her parents, and every day she told him another story about the olden days.

Best of all, Paul-Paul liked stories about unicorns. They were so wild and fierce and strong, and they galloped so fast, and they were the most beautiful of all the animals, Paul-Paul thought.

Every day he asked Marie-Céleste to tell him another story about them.

But the day came when Marie-Céleste had to go back to college in Paris, and Paul-Paul wouldn't see her again for a long time.

'But I've brought you a little present,' she said, when she came to say goodbye. 'Something to keep you company while I'm away.'

Paul-Paul's present was a big picture of a tapestry with a unicorn in it, which Marie-Céleste had cut out of a magazine and glued to a piece of cardboard. She put it on Paul-Paul's mantelpiece, where he could see it from his bed. There were lots of forest trees in the picture, as well as the unicorn, and the ground was covered with hundreds of little white flowers. On the ground in front of the unicorn knelt a young page-boy, who was holding out a bunch of flowers for the unicorn to sniff, as a way of taming him. And there were also lots of little birds, and rabbits, and squirrels, and foxes, and deer, peeping out from the leaves and undergrowth. Paul-Paul thought it was the best picture he had ever seen.

'There are lots of tapestries like that in a museum in Paris,' said Marie-Céleste. 'And one day, when you're well again, I'll take you to see them. So get well soon!'

After Marie-Céleste had gone away, Paul-Paul often lay and looked at his unicorn picture for a long time. The unicorn was very handsome, with his sharp white horn, and his long, white, wavy tail, and his white foreleg fiercely pawing the ground. Paul-Paul wished and wished that one day he would meet a unicorn, and tame it, just as the page-boy in the picture was doing.

Paul-Paul found that sometimes, if he gazed and gazed at the picture, blinking and blinking, his bedroom seemed to fade away, and he seemed to be in the tapestry forest himself. He seemed to have become the page-boy in the picture, and he seemed to be kneeling in front of the unicorn, holding out the bunch of little white flowers for him to sniff. And then, as he gazed and gazed, he felt as if he really was climbing on to the unicorn's back, and galloping away through the trees – far, far away, to the wildest

depths of the forest, with the sound of the unicorn's hoofs drumming in his ears, and the trees flashing past on either side . . .

When Paul-Paul was day-dreaming, as well as looking more like
an owl than ever, he was so far away in his mind that it was quite
hard to wake him up. 'Tuwit-tuwoo!' his mother would say,
laughing, as she stood by his bed with a tray in her hands. 'Here's
your supper, little owl! Wake up! Tuwit-tuwoo!'

Paul-Paul would wake up from his imaginary gallop in the
forest with a sigh. He wondered how much longer it would be
before he was well again, and could go for a long walk in the
real forest. He wondered, too, more and more, if there were any
unicorns there.

CHAPTER 2

Fleury-des-Bois

❧

PAUL-PAUL'S imaginary gallops on the unicorn's back must have done him more good than any medicine, because he soon began to get well again very quickly. And then at last the day came when he was allowed to get up, although he wasn't allowed to go back to school again straight away, and he still had to have a rest in the afternoons.

The first thing Paul-Paul wanted to do was to go for a long walk in the forest. But his mother shook her head, and said, 'It's much too far, and you're not nearly strong enough yet. We'll see how you are in a few weeks' time.'

The next thing Paul-Paul wanted to do was to explore Fleury-des-Bois, and get to know it again. This time his mother said yes, although she wouldn't let him go very far away, in case he got too tired. But Paul-Paul didn't mind. There was plenty to look at in the streets and lanes near his house.

Fleury-des-Bois was a very pretty village. The streets were cobbled, and all the houses had grey stone walls with bright red creeper growing on them, and brown tiled roofs, and shutters on all the windows. The gardens of the houses had high stone walls round them, and they were full of fruit-trees. It was autumn just at this time, and the fruit-trees leaned their heavy-laden branches over the tops of the walls, and dropped their ripe apples and pears and peaches and plums into the narrow back lanes which wound between the gardens. The fruit which fell there was free, and anyone could take it. Paul-Paul had a wonderful time, eating as much as he could pick up.

Fleury-des-Bois seemed just like a fairy-tale village to Paul-Paul. When he looked at the great forest rising beyond the rooftops and the fruit-trees, all beautifully red and gold with autumn leaves, he felt sure that there must be unicorns there.

This made him more anxious than ever to go for a long walk in the forest. So he spent every morning running as fast as he could up and down the streets and lanes near his house, to make his legs stronger. By lunch-time he was always very hungry, and wanted second helpings of everything.

Soon the doctor said that he was quite better, and could go back to school the next week.

'Then I must be well enough to go for a long walk in the forest!' Paul-Paul said eagerly to his mother, when the doctor had gone. 'Can we go this afternoon?'

'I shall be much too busy this afternoon, I'm afraid,' said his mother, 'You'd better ask your father.'

Paul-Paul asked his father, and then he asked his grandmother, and then he asked Rose-Marie, but they were all too busy; and Louis-Philippe was still away in the Army. Nor was Paul-Paul allowed to go to the forest by himself, in case he got lost.

'You'll just have to wait until someone has time to take you,' said his mother.

Paul-Paul knew what that meant. It meant that no one was *ever* going to have time to take him to the forest. He sighed, and wandered out into the back garden. After a while, he climbed up the pear-tree by the vegetable patch, and gazed wistfully over the top of the wall at the forest. How beautiful and mysterious it looked, with its tall trees rustling their leaves invitingly at him, and showering down catkins and acorns and conkers with every gust of wind, and its narrow paths winding far, far away into the mingled green, gold and brown undergrowth! The longer he gazed, the more sure he felt that there must be a unicorn lurking there somewhere, just out of sight. And yet now he might never see it, just because no one would take him to the forest.

Then Paul-Paul remembered Marie-Céleste. She wasn't like other grown-ups at all. She would have time to take him to the forest, and if there were unicorns there, she would know, and she would help him find one. If only she would come back soon!

*   *   *

Meanwhile, Paul-Paul started going to school again. The school was in the village square, where the shops and the church were. Paul-Paul had a lot of catching up to do, after being ill for so long, but he enjoyed the lessons, especially the lessons about plants and wild animals, which were called Science. But one day, in a Science lesson, something terrible happened.

They had been learning all about different kinds of horses, including zebras, and at the end of the lesson, as usual, they were allowed to ask questions. Paul-Paul, who had been hoping all through the lesson to hear about unicorns, put up his hand and asked, 'Please sir, aren't unicorns a sort of horse?'

'Unicorns?' said his teacher, bursting out laughing. 'Unicorns don't exist!'

'But there are lots of them in fairy-tales,' said Paul-Paul. 'Lots and lots of them!'

'But fairy-tales aren't true!' said his teacher, laughing more than ever. 'Oh, what a dreamy-head you are, Paul-Paul!'

By this time, all the other children in the class were laughing too. Unicorns didn't exist, and everyone was laughing at him! Paul-Paul hid his head under the flap of his desk, feeling as if the end of the world had come. And he stayed there, with his eyes shut tight, until everyone had stopped laughing.

By the time Paul-Paul came out from under his desk-lid, he had decided to go on believing in unicorns anyway, even if they didn't exist. And after this, he often daydreamed about them in class, instead of paying attention to the lesson. Then the teacher would ask him a question, and he wouldn't hear. 'Tuwit-tuwoo!' all the children in the class would start shouting. 'Wake up, Paul-Paul! Tuwit-tuwoo!'

But the more Paul-Paul was teased, the more he believed in unicorns. And sometimes, when he was daydreaming about them, a strange feeling crept over him. He *knew* that unicorns existed – he could *feel* that they did! Perhaps they didn't exist in the ordinary way that rabbits, for instance, existed; but perhaps they existed in some other, magic way, unknown to science? In that case, there must be some magic way of finding one – perhaps even in the forest next to the village – if he only knew how. More than

ever he wished that Marie-Céleste would come home, and explain
it all to him.

Meanwhile, Paul-Paul was still busy getting to know Fleury-des-
Bois again. Sometimes, after school, he walked right round the
village square before he went home, stopping to have a really
good look at everything.

The square was the most important part of Fleury-des-Bois. It
was in the middle of the village, and all the main streets led out
of it. On one side they led towards the forest, and on the other
side they led towards the open country and the farms. But
wherever people lived – even if they lived as far away as the
furthest farms – if they wanted to go shopping, or go to school,
or go to church, or meet their friends, they always came to the
village square. That was where everything happened.

When Paul-Paul walked round the square, the first thing he
came to was the Town Hall, which was next door to his school.
It was called the Mairie.

The Mairie was a big grey building, with wide stone steps
leading up to its important-looking doors. Over the doors were
some large letters carved in the stone. They spelt 'LIBERTÉ,
ÉGALITÉ, FRATERNITÉ', which is the motto of the French
people. Above the motto, on the top of the Mairie, was a flag-
pole, which flew the French flag on special occasions. The French
flag was called the Tricolore, and it was red, white and blue.

Sometimes, when Paul-Paul walked past the Mairie, the mayor
would be standing at the top of the steps, looking out at the
square. He was called Monsieur le Maire. He was a very fat man,
with round red cheeks, and a gold watch on a chain, which he
kept in his waistcoat pocket. Sometimes he let Paul-Paul look at
his watch, and listen to it ticking.

After the Mairie there were a lot of shops, which went round
two sides of the square. First there was a butcher's shop, called
the Boucherie, which had a lot of meat on a marble slab in the
window, and a beautiful red and white striped awning. Next there
was the baker's shop which belonged to Marie-Céleste's parents –
Paul-Paul's uncle, Oncle César, and his aunt, Tante Madeleine.

The baker's shop was called the Boulangerie, and it had all sorts of cakes and biscuits and pastries in the window. Sometimes Paul-Paul went in and asked Tante Madeleine, who served behind the counter, if Marie-Céleste was coming home soon. 'Not just yet, I'm afraid,' Tante Madeleine would say, and she would give Paul-Paul a biscuit or a gingerbread man to console him.

After the Boulangerie, there was a grocer's shop, called the Épicerie, which sold every kind of food you could think of except meat and bread and cakes. It even sold fruit and vegetables, which were on a stall outside the shop, on the pavement. And after the Épicerie there was a chemist's shop, called the Pharmacie, which had a big green neon sign in the shape of a cross hanging over the door. And then there was the Post Office, called the Bureau de Poste, where Paul-Paul's father went every day to collect the letters and parcels which he delivered to all the houses. And then there was the hairdresser's, called the Coiffeur de Dames, where Rose-Marie worked, and which had a pink smell. And at the end of the row of shops, on the corner, was a café, where Louis-Philippe went to meet his friends and play dice when he was home on leave. The café had a blue and orange striped awning, and some tables and chairs outside on the pavement. There were always a few people sitting there having their drinks out in the sun if it was a fine day, and watching the people go by. 'Bonjour, Paul-Paul!' they would say, when Paul-Paul went by.

On the fourth side of the square, all by itself, was the church, with the parish priest's little house joined on to it. It had big stone steps leading up to it, and sometimes, when Paul-Paul walked past, the parish priest would be standing at the top of the steps, looking out at the square. He was called Monsieur l'Abbé, and he was a little, round, smiling man, with a wide-brimmed black hat, and a long black coat with buttons all the way down the front. In his coat pocket he kept a lot of big, stripy peppermints, to give to any children he happened to meet. He always gave one to Paul-Paul whenever Paul-Paul walked by.

Paul-Paul liked Monsieur l'Abbé very much, and he often stopped to have a chat with him. Monsieur l'Abbé told him lots of stories about angels, and about saints who had made friends with wild animals and birds. But not even Monsieur l'Abbé believed in unicorns. Paul-Paul had asked him.

In the middle of the square there were some plane-trees and a war memorial. The war memorial was a tall pillar with lots of statues of soldiers carved on it, and a long list of names. They were the names of all the men of Fleury-des-Bois who had been soldiers in the last two wars, and had got killed in them. About half way down the list there was Paul-Paul's own grandfather. That was why Paul-Paul's grandmother lived with them.

Under the plane-trees in the middle of the square, there were green benches for the old people to sit on. There were also a great many pigeons, strutting about on the ground, or perching on the war memorial. Whenever the church bells rang, which was several times a day, up would fly all the pigeons in the square at once, with a great whirring of wings, and round and round they would all circle together above the rooftops, until the bells stopped ringing again. Paul-Paul loved to be standing in the middle of the square when all the pigeons flew up. It was just as if the grey paving-stones themselves had turned into a flock of birds, and were flying upwards. It made Paul-Paul feel as if he was flying himself.

Usually the village square was quite quiet and peaceful, except on Mondays. Monday was market-day in Fleury-des-Bois, and the market was held in the square.

On Monday mornings, very early, before it was light, the farmers and their families came in to Fleury-des-Bois from the country, and set up their stalls under the plane-trees. They sold fresh fruit and vegetables from their farms, and fresh eggs laid by their chickens, and fresh cheese and butter which they had made themselves with the milk from their cows. They also sold hams, and plucked chickens for roasting, and sausages. And as well as the farmers, other people came from faraway places, and set up their stalls in the square too. They sold fresh fish from the sea, and sweets, and boots and shoes, and clothes, and toys, and furniture. You could buy anything you could think of in the market in Fleury-des-Bois.

On market-day, everyone in Fleury-des-Bois came to the square,

to buy and sell, and meet all their friends, and chatter their heads off. The square was filled with jostling crowds, and shouting stallholders, and barking dogs, and children running about everywhere. It certainly wasn't quiet and peaceful then!

Nor was it quiet and peaceful on Sunday afternoons or on public holidays, for the village band would give a concert. Then everyone in Fleury-des-Bois came to listen. They strolled about under the plane-trees, or sat on the green benches and ate their picnic teas while they listened. The pigeons had a wonderful time waddling about under everyone's feet, pecking at all the crumbs of cake which people had dropped. There were always children marching about in time to the music, and sometimes, in the evening, there were fairy-lights in the plane-trees, and everyone danced.

The village band was a splendid sight, sitting in rows on the steps of the Mairie, with their smart crimson and gold uniforms, and their scarlet cheeks puffed out as they played, and the Tricolore flapping in the breeze above their heads. There was Monsieur le Maire himself conducting them, and Monsieur l'Abbé, still in his black hat and coat, playing the cornet, while Paul-Paul's teacher played the trombone. And there were also several trumpets, and French horns, and flutes, and saxophones, and piccolos, and, best of all, the big drum. It made Paul-Paul's heart nearly burst with excitement to listen.

Paul-Paul thought that Fleury-des-Bois must be the best village in the whole world. And when the band was playing, and there were fairy-lights in the plane-trees, and everyone was dancing, he felt more sure than ever that unicorns existed somewhere, in some magic way.

'If only Marie-Céleste would come home, and help me find one,' thought Paul-Paul, 'then everything would be perfect.'

CHAPTER 3

At the Boulangerie

♣

NOW that Paul-Paul was back at school, his mother sometimes sent him on shopping errands to the village square.

One winter day, after school, she sent him to the Boulangerie, to buy some cakes for tea. Paul-Paul loved going to buy cakes, although it also made him feel a bit sad, because Marie-Céleste was never there.

But when Paul-Paul went into the Boulangerie that afternoon, he got a big surprise. Instead of Tante Madeleine standing behind the counter, there was Marie-Céleste herself! Paul-Paul could hardly believe his eyes. 'You're back!' he cried. 'No one told me!'

'I only came back last night,' said Marie-Céleste. 'I was going to come and see you this evening, as soon as the shops shut, as a surprise. But what a surprise *you* are!' she added, looking Paul-Paul up and down admiringly. 'I'd heard you were better – but how tall and strong you look now! I hardly recognized you.'

Just then, a customer came into the shop, and asked for some cakes. Paul-Paul watched Marie-Céleste lift the cakes from their trays with a pair of little silver tongs, and put them in a white cardboard box. Then she took the money, rang up the amount on the cash register with a ping, and gave the customer some change, saying, 'Merci, Madame! Au revoir, Madame!' just as Tante Madeleine always did.

'Where's Tante Madeleine?' asked Paul-Paul, after the customer had gone.

'She's ill in bed, I'm afraid,' said Marie-Céleste. 'She hasn't been too well for some time, you know, and now the doctor says she must stay in bed and have a long rest. That's why I've come home. I'm going to be working in the shop every day from now on, and I shan't be going back to college any more.'

Paul-Paul couldn't help thinking that this was the best news he had heard for a long time. Now he would be able to see Marie-Céleste as often as he liked. He would be able to go for long walks with her in the forest, and maybe even hunt for unicorns. He was just going to ask her how soon they could go to the forest when several more customers came into the shop. Marie-Céleste was busy serving them for quite a long time. Paul-Paul began to realize that she was probably going to be too busy now to take him to the forest, just as everyone else was. She might even be too busy to talk to him.

'You *are* going to be busy,' he said, rather sadly, when she had finished serving the customers, and was neatly rearranging the cakes on their shelves, and sweeping up some crumbs on the floor, while she waited for some more customers to come in.

'Very,' agreed Marie-Céleste. 'I shall have my mother to nurse, and the shop to mind, and all the cooking and housework to do as well. I don't suppose I shall have a day off for weeks.'

When Paul-Paul heard this, he knew it was no use even asking about walks in the forest, or talks about unicorns. He bought the cakes his mother had sent him to buy, and began to turn sadly away. Some more customers had already come in, and he thought he would just be a nuisance if he stayed in the shop any longer.

As Paul-Paul was leaving the shop, he noticed that a stray dog had sneaked in while the door was open, and was just going to steal a bun from a low shelf by the window. Marie-Céleste was so busy serving her customers that she hadn't even noticed. 'Shoo!' Paul-Paul cried, waving his arms at the dog, and it scuttled off quickly out of the shop.

'Oh, Paul-Paul, thank you!' said Marie-Céleste. 'That blessed dog! It's stolen two buns today already!'

This gave Paul-Paul an idea. 'I could come and help you in the shop after school, sometimes, if you like,' he said. 'I could chase away dogs, and sweep the floor for you, and run errands.'

'That would be a great help,' said Marie-Céleste. 'Could you really?'

'I'll come back tomorrow,' promised Paul-Paul. And he skipped all the way across the square on his way home. He thought that it would be fun to help Marie-Céleste in the shop. And if he worked hard, there might even be time to talk about unicorns after all.

The next day, after school, Paul-Paul started work at the Boulangerie, instead of playing in the back lanes with the other children, as he usually did. Soon he was calling in there for a little while nearly every day.

Marie-Céleste gave him lots of jobs to do. As well as shooing away stray dogs, and sweeping the floor, he counted the money in the cash register for her, and sometimes he even minded the shop for a few minutes all by himself, while Marie-Céleste went upstairs to see if her mother needed anything.

Paul-Paul's favourite job was selling the bread. French loaves are very long and thin. Some of them were so long that they were taller than Paul-Paul when they were standing upright, which was how they were kept while they were waiting to be sold, propped up in a wooden rack along one side of the shop. It was Paul-Paul's job to pull a long loaf out of the rack when a customer asked for one. This saved Marie-Céleste from having to come out from behind the counter. Soon the customers didn't even ask Marie-Céleste for their bread when Paul-Paul was there. They would buy their cakes from her, and then they would say, 'And one loaf of bread, please, Paul-Paul!' When other children came to the shop to buy bread for their mothers, Paul-Paul couldn't help feeling very superior to them. They were only customers, while he worked there!

In the Boulangerie, there was always a lovely smell of baking bread coming up from the cellar, where fat Oncle César worked all day, baking dozens and dozens of long loaves in the big ovens. Sometimes, when Paul-Paul was there, Oncle César would come puffing and staggering up the stairs from the cellar, carrying a big basket full of crisp, hot, golden loaves, which he had just taken out of the ovens. 'Here's some more work for you, Paul-Paul!' he would say, dumping the big basket down on the floor at Paul-Paul's feet. And it was Paul-Paul's job to take the new loaves out of the basket and put them in the rack.

When it was time for Paul-Paul to go home, Marie-Céleste would give him a loaf of bread to take with him, if his mother had asked him to bring one. But when he offered Marie-Céleste the money which his mother had given him to pay for it, she always refused to take it. 'No, no!' she would say. 'You've worked hard, and you've earned it.'

At supper, when Paul-Paul was sitting with his family round the kitchen table with its red check tablecloth, and his father was cutting the bread, and everyone was taking a slice, Paul-Paul felt very proud and important. It was he who had earned the bread which his family was eating!

Paul-Paul enjoyed helping at the Boulangerie so much that he almost forgot about unicorns. And even when he did remember them, he and Marie-Céleste were far too busy to talk. No sooner had they finished serving one customer, than another always came in.

But one day, in the middle of winter, Paul-Paul went to the Boulangerie much later than usual, because he had had some homework to do first. The shops were still open, but it was getting dark already, and there were very few people about. Most of them had finished their shopping by then, and gone home.

When Paul-Paul went into the Boulangerie, there was no one in the shop. He wondered where Marie-Céleste could have gone. Then he saw that a door behind the counter, which had always been shut before, was open. And there was Marie-Céleste in the room beyond, bending over a table with her back to the door, working at something. 'Come in here, Paul-Paul!' she called over her shoulder. 'Come and see what I'm doing.'

Paul-Paul went round behind the counter and into the room where Marie-Céleste was working. It was the funniest room Paul-Paul had ever seen. It was small, and round, and it had a high, pointed roof. 'It used to be the old baking-house, hundreds of years ago,' Marie-Céleste explained. 'And that,' she went on, pointing up at the high, pointed roof, 'was the chimney. But now I'm using it as my pastry-kitchen. Look!' And she showed Paul-Paul the table in the middle of the room which she had been working at.

On the table were dozens and dozens of cakes, which she had just finished making. There were rows and rows of jam tarts, and chocolate éclairs, and macaroons, and cream slices, and rum babas, and doughnuts, and florentines, and all sorts of lovely fruit flans and different kinds of biscuits. It was what Marie-Céleste had been learning to do at college in Paris.

'Well, that's one lot finished!' said Marie-Céleste, dusting the pastry-flour off her fingers. 'Now for the next lot! Would you like to give me a hand?'

'Oh yes!' said Paul-Paul.

So Paul-Paul got to work whisking eggs with an egg-whisk, and stirring the big bowls of cake-mix with a wooden spoon, and then pouring in the currants, and the candied peel, and the angelica, and the glacé cherries, and the chopped walnuts, while Marie-Céleste did the stirring. Then he helped her put all the cakes on special wire trays, and watched her slide the trays carefully into the pastry-oven, which was in one corner of the room. And then, a little while later, he helped her take them out of the oven again when they were cooked – all piping hot, and smelling like a meadow full of summer flowers. And after this there was still all the icing to make, and the cream to whip, and the fruit to be put in the fruit flans.

When they had finished, and Paul-Paul had scraped out all the bowls, and licked all the spoons, it was time to arrange the cakes on the shelves in the shop window. It all looked so delicious that they went outside and stood on the pavement looking in at their window display, just as if they were customers themselves.

'You *have* worked hard!' said Marie-Céleste. 'You'd better choose a cake for yourself, as a reward.'

Paul-Paul looked at all the cakes in the window, wondering which to choose. And then suddenly he noticed a little strawberry flan sitting all by itself in the corner of the window, as if it had been forgotten. It had the plumpest and juiciest strawberries of all in it, and the biggest dollop of whipped cream on top. Paul-Paul saw that Marie-Céleste was smiling.

'I'll have that one!' he said.

After this, Paul-Paul often went to the Boulangerie in the evening, and helped Marie-Céleste make cakes. But even better than that, he loved to watch her icing birthday cakes and wedding cakes, which she also did in the evenings, when there weren't a lot of customers.

By this time, people from miles around were ordering their wedding cakes and birthday cakes from Marie-Céleste. There was no one else in all that part of the country who was as clever as

she was at decorating a cake with silver bells and silver horseshoes, and candles of all different colours, and pink and blue ribbons tied in little bows, and patterns made of icing sugar. Sometimes the icing sugar patterns looked just like the finest lace, and sometimes like a lattice on a garden wall, complete with leaves and flowers. If it was a wedding cake, Marie-Céleste would add little sugar rosebuds and bluebirds. And if it was a birthday cake, she would add little dogs and cats and rabbits and teddy bears, dancing hand in hand round the sides, all made of different coloured icing sugar. And on top of the cake, in beautiful curly writing, she would put 'Joyeuse Anniversaire!', which means 'Happy Birthday' in French.

It was very peaceful in the little pastry-kitchen in the evenings, and very cosy too, from the warmth of the pastry-oven. Outside, in the dark square, snow was falling, and they were very seldom disturbed by a customer. There was plenty of time to talk at last.

The conversation soon came round to the olden days, and legends about magic forests, which Marie-Céleste liked talking about just as much as Paul-Paul did. But now that Paul-Paul at last had a chance to ask her about unicorns, he felt almost afraid to, in case she too said that they didn't exist. If *she* said so, then it would really be true that they didn't. But in the end he could bear the suspense no longer, and asked, 'Do unicorns exist, Marie-Céleste?'

Marie-Céleste added a rosebud to the wedding cake she was icing in a thoughtful silence.

'Well, I don't know if they exist now,' she said at last, 'but I think they must have existed in the olden days. Otherwise why should there be so many legends about them, and so many unicorns in old tapestries? Nowadays people say those legends aren't true, but perhaps the world was just quite different in the olden days. There wasn't so much science then, but perhaps there was much more magic. And the forests were much bigger and wilder and darker in those days too. I expect people saw all sorts of strange, magic creatures which we never see.'

'But why did the world change?' asked Paul-Paul sadly.

'Because people started believing in science instead of in magic,

I suppose,' said Marie-Céleste. 'And I think that when people stop believing in it, magic just goes away.'

'Then I'll never see a unicorn!' said Paul-Paul in despair.

Marie-Céleste looked up from icing the wedding cake with a smile. 'Never say never!' she said. 'Miracles do happen!' And she went on, adding a bluebird to the wedding cake, 'If you believed in magic enough, it might come back again, mightn't it?'

This conversation gave Paul-Paul a great deal to think about. It seemed to him that the only way to find a unicorn was either to get back into the olden days, or make the olden days come back into the present time. He couldn't think how to do either of these things, except by believing and hoping and wishing with all his might. He tried this lots of times, especially at night, when he was lying in bed looking at his unicorn picture by the glow of his night-light, and waiting to go to sleep. But nothing happened. Perhaps he wasn't believing hard enough?

One day, when winter was nearly over, and spring was coming, he asked Marie-Céleste, '*How* do you believe in magic enough to make it happen?'

'Well, I think it was going for long walks in the forest which made me believe in magic,' said Marie-Céleste. 'It's easy to believe in magic there. I suppose that's because the forest hasn't changed much since the olden days. Have you tried doing that?'

'I've never been to the forest,' said Paul-Paul. 'No one has ever had time to take me – not even you!'

'Oh, Paul-Paul!' said Marie-Céleste. 'How awful! Well, we must certainly put that right.' She thought for a moment, and then said, 'Now that my mother's nearly better, perhaps she'd mind the shop for me one afternoon, so that I could take you there. Yes, I'm sure she would. What about next Saturday?'

CHAPTER 4

The forest

♣

PAUL-PAUL thought Saturday would never come, the time passed so slowly, but at last it did. It was a beautiful sunny day, the first fine day for weeks. The sky was a very pale blue, with little wispy clouds high up in it, being chased about by a soft, warm breeze. All the fruit-trees in the walled gardens in Fleury-des-Bois were coming out into pretty pink and white blossom. After lunch, Paul-Paul leapt and danced about in his garden, while he waited for Marie-Céleste to come and fetch him. He was so excited he couldn't keep still.

At last she arrived, and they set off along the road which led away from Paul-Paul's house into the forest, winding uphill all the way. Then, after a while, they came to a little path which turned off from the road, and led to the wildest depths of the forest.

It was a very narrow path, so narrow that they had to walk in single file. Marie-Céleste led the way. Paul-Paul's eyes grew very wide as he followed her deeper and deeper into the thick, dark undergrowth. Brambles clutched at his clothes and his hair, and there were strange rustlings in the bushes, and sudden twitterings of birds. The branches met overhead, and it seemed to grow darker every moment. Once a wood-pigeon suddenly flew up from a bush beside Paul-Paul, making him nearly jump out of his skin. It flapped away through the trees, its wings making a noise like a witch's cackling laughter in the gloom ahead of them. Paul-Paul began to wonder if he really wanted to go to the wildest depths of the forest after all.

Then suddenly Marie-Céleste stopped still, and Paul-Paul gave a gasp. The thick undergrowth had ended, and they were standing at the edge of a great stretch of open woodland. The tall forest trees stretched away into the distance as far as Paul-Paul could see, as solemn and beautiful as the columns and arches in a cathedral. The air between them was a dim green twilight, and the ground beneath them was covered with thousands and thousands of flowers like little white stars.

'Marie-Céleste!' cried Paul-Paul. 'It's just like my unicorn picture!'

He ran about this way and that between the trees, picking the little white flowers. And then he ran back to Marie-Céleste with a bunch of them in his hand, to show them to her. They were prettier than ever when you looked at them closely, for there were tiny purple veins in their white petals, so fine that you could hardly see them. 'What are they called?' Paul-Paul asked.

'They're wood anemones,' said Marie-Céleste. 'But we call them passion-flowers, because they always come out at this time of the year, during Holy Week.'

Marie-Céleste and Paul-Paul walked on, stepping carefully between the passion-flowers, so as not to tread on any of them. Paul-Paul was still carrying his bunch, to take home with him. Soon he found other spring flowers – blue periwinkles and violets, and primroses, and celandines hiding in the lush grass and leaves wherever the ground was damp.

The open forest went on and on. Sometimes the ground sloped gently up to sun-dappled hilltops, and then down again into shadowy hollows full of brambles and last autumn's dead leaves. But gradually the sunny hilltops grew fewer, and the shadowy hollows grew deeper, and darker, and more frequent, until they seemed to be walking downhill nearly all the time. They seemed to be going down into a deep, deep valley.

Soon the undergrowth was so thick and tangled that they had to walk in single file again. It was very creepy. The trees were covered with ivy, which looped its long tendrils across the path, and the stones underfoot were slippery with moss. There were great, grey, strangely-shaped boulders amongst the bracken and brambles, which looked just like lurking wolves at first sight. Once they passed a high cliff of grey rock, whose face was curtained with ivy. At its foot there was the dark opening of a cave, and on the ground outside the cave there were some blood-stained feathers and some bones.

'What sort of animal lives there?' whispered Paul-Paul, his heart beating fast.

'Only a fox,' said Marie-Céleste. 'Those look like chicken feathers to me.'

All the same, Paul-Paul couldn't help giving a shiver as he looked back at the cave, and he wondered more than ever if he really wanted to go to the wildest depths of the forest.

But then something happened which made him forget all his fears. Suddenly a rabbit shot out from the bracken just at his feet, and bounded away through the undergrowth. And a moment later he saw a squirrel leaping from branch to branch among the trees ahead. Soon every clearing they passed was abob with the white tails of rabbits running away at their approach, and the branches of all the trees seemed to be alive with leaping squirrels. Wood-pigeons and other birds flew up from almost every bush, and once they even saw a beautiful red-gold fox loping away into the undergrowth. If only they would stay, and let him make friends with them!

'Why are there so many wild animals just here?' he cried in wonder.

'You'll know why in a minute,' said Marie-Céleste, with a mysterious smile. 'Run on ahead and you'll see.'

Paul-Paul ran on ahead, and as soon as he was round the next bend in the path, he found himself standing at the edge of a beautiful big pool, almost as big as a lake. Willows and hazels overhung the water, and there were bulrushes and yellow irises growing in the shallows at the margin. Further out, the round leaves of wild water-lilies mottled the surface. And on the far shore, the ground began to slope up again, still covered with the same tangle of trees, rocks and bracken – up and up to the distant wooded skyline. They were at the bottom of the deep valley. Perhaps they were at the very centre of the whole forest!

By the time Paul-Paul had taken it all in, Marie-Céleste was at

2

his side. 'Now you see why there are so many wild animals just here,' she said. 'Animals need water to drink just as we do, and there are very few streams or pools in the forest. So when they find a big pool like this, they make their homes near it, so that they'll never be thirsty.'

Then Marie-Céleste showed Paul-Paul all the different animals' footprints in the mud and sand at the water's edge, where they had come down to drink. She taught Paul-Paul how to recognize all the different footprints. But there was one kind of footprint, a little bigger than the rest, which she refused to explain to him. 'Wait and see!' she said, with another mysterious smile. 'If we're lucky, and keep very quiet, we might see the animals which made those.'

Paul-Paul didn't think it could possibly be a unicorn, and he wondered what other sort of animal it could be. But there wasn't any other animal he could think of.

Meanwhile, they sat down side by side on a fallen tree-trunk

close to the pool to wait. There was plenty to look at. There were dragonflies hovering about among the rushes and irises, like little bright blue or bright green helicopters. And there were the first spring butterflies too, a velvety golden brown, fluttering about among the scented bushes beside the pool. There was even a little green frog sitting sunning himself on a water-lily leaf, as still as a tiny green statue – so still that it was quite a long time before Marie-Céleste and Paul-Paul noticed him. But even after they had, he went on sunning himself just as before, not knowing that they were looking at him, or not minding.

But then, all of a sudden, the little frog dived into the water with a plop. Something had startled him, and it hadn't been Marie-Céleste or Paul-Paul, for they had been sitting perfectly quiet and still. Then Paul-Paul heard a faint rustling in the bracken on the far side of the pool, and looked up. Marie-Céleste put her finger to her lips to warn him not to make a sound.

For there, stepping delicately out from the bracken, and coming

down to the water's edge to drink, was a herd of wild deer. There was a stag, with great branching antlers, and several does, and one little fawn. They all had golden-brown coats with white dapples on them, and beautiful wide dark eyes. The handsome stag kept watch while the does and the fawn went down into the shallows and bent their heads to drink. The little fawn, who was still young enough to be rather wobbly on his legs, kept close to his mother. He frisked a little in the shallows, and then bent his head and snorted into the water instead of drinking it, splashing his mother's face. Paul-Paul found it very difficult not to laugh.

Meanwhile the stag stood with his splendid head raised, looking slowly and watchfully all round the margin of the pool. Gradually his head turned until he was looking straight at Marie-Céleste and Paul-Paul. And then his eyes widened suddenly, and he gave a sharp little snort. At once, the drinking does lifted their heads, wheeled round in the shallows with a splash, and stampeded off into the bracken, the little fawn scampering at his mother's side. The stag stood bravely facing Marie-Céleste and Paul-Paul, his head bent and his fierce antlers pointing at them, guarding the retreat of the herd. And then, when the does and the fawn had vanished safely into the bracken, he too turned, and with one great bound he disappeared.

Paul-Paul stood up to watch the deer go. But already they were nowhere to be seen. The trees and undergrowth were not at all dense on the far side of the pool, and he couldn't understand how it was the deer had vanished so quickly. They seemed to have simply melted into the rocks and the bracken and the silver birches, as if by magic. And then all at once he caught sight of them again, winding in single file along a narrow path, already half way up the opposite hillside. Their golden brown coats were so exactly the same colour as the dead bracken, and their white dapples were so like the grey rocks and the trunks of the silver birches, that he would never have noticed them if he hadn't been looking for them, and they hadn't been moving.

'I thought we'd see them,' said Marie-Céleste. 'It's been a warm day, so they were bound to be thirsty. And it's usually at this time of day – just before sunset – that animals come to drink. And the wind has dropped too, so that they couldn't scent us.' And then she asked with a smile, 'Was that nearly as good as seeing a unicorn?'

Paul-Paul nodded happily. 'I didn't know there were any wild deer in the forest nowadays,' he said. 'I thought they belonged to the olden days, like unicorns.'

Seeing the deer had made Paul-Paul feel just as if he was back in the olden days. And the way the deer had melted into the rocks and bracken, becoming quite invisible, made it very easy to believe in magic. There was a pussy-willow tree leaning out over the pool, its branches all silvery-white with little silky purses. Paul-Paul found that if he half-closed his eyes, it was easy to imagine that it was a unicorn in disguise, bending his white neck to drink.

How close the olden days seemed, and all their magic, here in the forest! Paul-Paul gazed dreamily into the pool. It looked just like a tapestry, with the rocks, and the bracken, and the silver birches, and the deer grazing on the far hillside, all reflected in the dark green water. The ripples even made all the reflections look as if they had been sewn with lots and lots of tiny stitches. Some of the reflections of the rocks, quivering deep in the centre of the pool, looked just like the pale turrets of a castle. Surely, if he only gazed long enough, and deeply enough, the reflections would become real, and he would find himself back in the olden days, walking towards that castle?

'Tuwit-tuwoo, Paul-Paul!' said Marie-Céleste. 'We've got to go home now, I'm afraid. It's getting late.'

'Oh, wait a minute!' cried Paul-Paul. For he had just seen a beautiful golden glow in the depths of the pool, like lamplight shining from a turret window. The reflections *were* coming to life, and he *was* nearly back in the olden days!

'Paul-Paul!' said Marie-Céleste, laughing, and pulling him away from the pool by his hand. 'We'll come back another time, I promise. But if we don't go now, we'll be caught in the forest in the dark.'

Paul-Paul looked up, and saw that the sun was setting. The golden glow in the pool had only been the reflection of the sunset sky. But all the same, he felt sure that if he could only have stayed longer, the magic would really have happened.

Meanwhile, the shadows were already very long and dark, and several bushes near the pool had begun to look black and sinister. Paul-Paul suddenly found that it was very easy to believe in dragons when you were in the forest, as well as in unicorns! 'Quick, quick!' he cried, and now it was he who was tugging Marie-Céleste along by the hand. The sooner they were safely home the better!

Back they scrambled up the steep, slippery path through the undergrowth. Under the tunnel of branches it was already nearly dark, and long tendrils of ivy trailed invisible, ghostly fingers across their faces. Paul-Paul held Marie-Céleste's hand tightly all the way, and pulled her up the steep path as fast as he could, especially when they had to pass the big grey cliff with the cave at its foot. It was all too easy to believe, now, that it was a dragon's lair! Paul-Paul wouldn't let Marie-Céleste stop for breath even when they were safely past it, not even when they had reached the open woodland again, although there was a lovely purple mist between the trees there, and the passion-flowers gleamed more whitely than ever. He didn't let her stop until they had scrambled through the last stretch of bushes and under-growth, and burst out into the open road.

The warm lights of Fleury-des-Bois looked very welcoming in the dusk. Paul-Paul waited until Marie-Céleste had got her breath back, and then they ran all the way down to his house for supper.

Paul-Paul had carried his bunch of passion-flowers all the way home, and before he went to bed that night he put them on his mantelpiece next to his unicorn picture, in a glass of water.

When he was in bed, he lay looking at the passion-flowers and the unicorn picture by the light of his night-light, and thinking about his walk in the forest, and especially about the pool and its mysterious reflections. He still felt sure that he had been very close to getting back into the olden days, when he was gazing into the pool. If only he could have stayed longer! But perhaps Marie-Céleste would be able to take him there again very soon.

Then Paul-Paul shut his eyes tight, and wished harder than he ever had before that he would meet a unicorn – if possible the very next weekend.

CHAPTER 5

Jean-Pierre

♣

BUT the next weekend was Easter, and Marie-Céleste was even busier than usual, selling hot cross buns and Easter eggs as well as all her usual cakes and bread. There was no time for another walk in the forest, but Paul-Paul didn't mind. Something happened that weekend which made him forget about unicorns for quite a long time.

On Easter Sunday Paul-Paul and his family went to church. Mass on Easter Sunday was a special occasion, like Christmas, and the church was beautifully decorated with flowers, and full of brightly glowing candles, and everyone wore their best clothes. The church was also very crowded, because lots of people who had gone away from Fleury-des-Bois to work or study in Paris came home for the holiday, and other people had friends or relations staying with them. So there were lots of new faces to look at.

After Paul-Paul and his family had arrived at the church, and were waiting for Mass to begin, Paul-Paul looked round to see what new faces he could see. And straight away he saw a tall and very handsome young man, whom he had never seen before, on the other side of the aisle. With his fair hair, and his bright blue eyes, he looked just like a prince, Paul-Paul thought. And there was also a carefree twinkle in his eyes, which made him look as if he would always be ready for a joke, or a game, or an adventure. Paul-Paul wished he could get to know him, and wondered very much who he was.

Just as Paul-Paul was wondering this, he overheard two old ladies in the pew in front of him whispering behind their veils. Paul-Paul knew them well. They were sisters, and they lived in a house in his street, and neither of them had ever been married. One was called Mademoiselle Augustine, and the other was called Mademoiselle Ernestine.

'Who's that fine-looking young man over there, next to Monsieur Dupré, the miller?' whispered Mademoiselle Ernestine, who was small, and plump, and timid.

'Why, that's Jean-Pierre Dupré, his son, of course!' whispered Mademoiselle Augustine, who was tall, and thin, and very bad-tempered. 'Really, Ernestine, you've no memory at all! Don't you remember, he went away into the Army a few years ago. He must have come home on leave.'

'How tall and handsome he's grown!' whispered Mademoiselle Ernestine, with a flutter. 'And one day he'll inherit the mill from his father, too, and be quite a rich man. What a fine husband he'll make for one of our girls!'

'Hm! If he's steady! Which I doubt!' whispered Mademoiselle Augustine, with a sniff. 'Don't you remember, he and his friend Alphonse Duval were the two naughtiest boys in the village when they were younger. Always climbing over people's garden walls and stealing their peaches, and plaguing everyone with their booby-traps and their stink-bombs! And that Jean-Pierre always tearing round corners on that bicycle of his, frightening old ladies out of their wits!' And she added sternly, 'You've got a mind like a sieve, Ernestine, and you're far too easily charmed by good looks!'

'But perhaps Army life has quietened him down,' whispered Mademoiselle Ernestine timidly.

'Hm! If it hasn't made him twenty times worse!' replied Mademoiselle Augustine, with a snort.

After hearing all this, Paul-Paul looked round and gazed at Jean-Pierre Dupré more admiringly than ever. More than ever he longed to get to know him, and he hoped very much that the Army *hadn't* quietened him down!

And then the little bell tinkled, and Mass began.

Paul-Paul hoped to see Jean-Pierre again at the end of Mass, but he lost sight of him in the crowd going out of the church. And by the time Paul-Paul had come out into the square, the Dupré family was nowhere to be seen. Paul-Paul knew that the mill was out in the country, quite a long way from Fleury-des-Bois. Monsieur and Madame Dupré and Jean-Pierre must have already set off for home.

Later that day the village band gave a concert, and the day after was market-day. The square was even more crowded than usual on both these occasions. But although Paul-Paul looked round everywhere for Jean-Pierre, there was no sign of him. Nor was there any sign of him during the days which followed. 'He must have gone back to the Army already,' thought Paul-Paul sadly, 'and now I shan't see him again.'

A week or so passed. And then, one day, when Paul-Paul was helping Marie-Céleste in the Boulangerie after school as usual, they heard an unusual and alarming sound. A lorry was coming roaring very fast through the narrow streets towards the square. As it came closer, Marie-Céleste and Paul-Paul could hear the squawking of chickens scuttling out of the way, and the wild barking of dogs, and loud toot-toots of the lorry's hooter, and shriekings of tyres as it came round corners too fast. And then all the pigeons in the square flapped up startled into the air; and with a squealing of brakes, and an extra loud toot-toot of greeting, a big, bright blue lorry pulled up outside the Boulangerie. On the side of the lorry, in big yellow letters, was written 'MOULIN DUPRÉ', and out of the driver's seat jumped Jean-Pierre himself!

Jean-Pierre opened the door of the Boulangerie with a clang. He was streaked with white flour from head to foot. 'Bonjour, Messieurs, Mesdames!' he called out in a cheerful, workmanlike voice. 'Your weekly delivery of flour from the Moulin Dupré has arrived!'

There were several customers in the Boulangerie, all standing stock still, as if they had been turned to stone by the commotion of Jean-Pierre's arrival. They blocked Jean-Pierre's view of Marie-Céleste behind the counter, so that he couldn't see her at all. But he saw Paul-Paul, who was near the door, and who happened to be handing a long loaf to a customer just at that moment, and taking the money for it, which he was now allowed to do.

'Ah, *there* you are!' said Jean-Pierre, bending down and offering a floury hand to Paul-Paul, with a teasing twinkle in his eye. 'You are, I presume, Monsieur Dubois, the baker?'

'No, I'm not! I'm Paul-Paul Dupont!' said Paul-Paul, laughing. 'Don't be silly!'

By this time, the customers who were standing in the way had all backed to the sides of the shop, leaving a space down the middle so that Jean-Pierre could see Marie-Céleste. 'My father will be up from the cellar in a moment,' she said, laughing at Jean-Pierre's joke.

When Jean-Pierre saw her, a sudden change came over him. The smile faded from his face, and his eyes seemed to become bluer than ever, and yet at the same time very dreamy, as if he had fallen under a magic spell. Paul-Paul guessed at once why he was looking like that. He was thinking that Marie-Céleste was the prettiest girl he had ever seen!

For a moment, Jean-Pierre stood very still, gazing at Marie-Céleste, as if he too had been turned to stone. And then he bent his head, and rubbed his forehead with his fist, and wiped his floury feet on the doormat, as if he was trying to tidy himself up. As Paul-Paul watched him, he suddenly thought that if ever a unicorn wanted to disappear by turning into a person, Jean-Pierre was what that unicorn would look like. His fist, as he rubbed his forehead, was like a unicorn's horn, and his foot, as he wiped it on the doormat, was like a unicorn's foreleg fiercely pawing the ground! And that was the last time Paul-Paul thought about unicorns for a long time.

Meanwhile Marie-Céleste, who was also looking rather strange and dreamy, called down the stairs to the cellar, 'Papa! The flour's come from the mill!'

After a moment, Oncle César came up from the cellar, wiping his hands on his big striped apron. 'Bonjour, Jean-Pierre!' he said, shaking hands with him. 'Helping your father while you're on leave?'

'No, I'm home for good, to work at the mill and learn the business,' said Jean-Pierre. 'My father has hurt his back, and wants to retire quite soon, and then I'm to run the mill myself.'

'Ah, settling down, eh?' said Oncle César.

'I suppose so,' said Jean-Pierre, sounding rather sad at having come to the end of his travels and adventures as a soldier.

'Well, let's get that flour unloaded!' said Oncle César, and he and Jean-Pierre went out of the shop. Paul-Paul went with them. He wanted to see the flour being unloaded. And Marie-Céleste quickly finished serving her last customer, and then came to the shop doorway to watch too.

Jean-Pierre helped Oncle César open the big wooden trap-door in the pavement outside the Boulangerie, which had a wooden chute running straight down to the cellar beneath. And then he leapt up on to the back of the lorry as deftly as an acrobat, and balanced there on the top of a pile of big plump sacks. 'Ready?' he called out. And then he began to throw down the heavy sacks of flour one by one to the pavement below, while Oncle César dragged them to the open trap-door, and slid them down the slippery wooden chute to the cellar.

At first, Jean-Pierre waited for Oncle César to push each sack down the chute before he threw the next. But soon he began to throw the sacks down faster and faster, with a cry of 'Op-là!' as he threw each one, tossing them down as if they were the lightest of feather pillows, and he was having a pillow fight instead of unloading a lorry. As each sack hit the pavement, out flew a great cloud of white dust, which swirled up into the air round Jean-Pierre like smoke in the sunlight, turning his dark blue overalls pale blue, and his fair hair almost white. But the more covered with dust he became, the more fun he seemed to be having.

Thud! Thud! Thud! went the sacks of flour all over the pavement. And then, 'Op-là!' Thud! A big sack landed right beside Paul-Paul, making him nearly jump out of his skin. Then 'Op-là!' Thud! And an even bigger sack landed with a bang close behind Oncle César, just as he was bending over the trap-door to slide another sack down the chute, and made him very nearly topple head-first down the chute himself.

'Eh, eh, eh!' cried Oncle César, laughing, when he had recovered his balance. 'Not so close! Not so fast!'

'Not so fast?' said Jean-Pierre. 'But your workman isn't helping you – that's why you can't keep up. Hey, you, young Monsieur Paul-Paul Dupont!' he called to Paul-Paul. 'Why aren't you giving your boss a hand?'

At this, Paul-Paul quickly took hold of a big sack, and tried to drag it towards the trap-door. He had been longing to be allowed to help. But though he pulled and pulled with all his might, the big sack wouldn't move an inch. It might just as well have been glued to the pavement.

'I can't,' Paul-Paul said sadly to Jean-Pierre, when he was quite out of breath from trying. 'It's too heavy.'

'Never mind!' said Jean-Pierre, who had been watching him from the top of the lorry with a smile. 'Try this one!' And then 'Op-là!' Plop! And a little sack of Marie-Céleste's fine pastry-flour landed at Paul-Paul's feet. This one was just the right size for Paul-Paul, and he dragged it happily across the pavement to the trap-door, then watched it slide with a whoosh down the chute into the darkness below. And no sooner had he straightened up than 'Op-là!' Plop! – another little sack of pastry-flour landed at his feet, and then a third, and a fourth, and a fifth. Paul-Paul was kept just as busy as Oncle César himself, rushing backwards and forwards across the pavement with the little sacks of pastry-flour, trying very hard to keep up with Jean-Pierre.

Soon all the sacks of flour had been thrown down from the lorry, and slid down the chute into the cellar. The clouds of white dust began to thin out and drift away in the breeze, and Oncle César, and Paul-Paul, and Jean-Pierre, who had jumped down from the back of the lorry, stood together on the pavement, gasping for breath and glowing from the hard work, while Marie-Céleste watched with a smile from the shop doorway. Paul-Paul, who was gasping and glowing just as much as Oncle César and Jean-Pierre were, and was just as covered with white dust from head to foot, felt like a real workman.

'Well, well! We've done that job in half the time it usually takes,' said Oncle César, while they were all slapping each other on the back, as real workmen always do. 'If you go on working at that pace, Jean-Pierre, you'll soon be a rich man. That is,' he added, 'if you don't frighten all your customers to death first!'

'It's Paul-Paul's mother who's going to have a fit when she sees him!' said Marie-Céleste, laughing at the sight of Paul-Paul's white clothes and white hair.

'Don't you worry, I'll soon get him clean!' said Jean-Pierre. And he began to tousle Paul-Paul's hair, and rumple his clothes, until they were more or less back to their usual colour. Then he said, 'Well, I must go. See you next Thursday.' And he began to walk towards the lorry.

By this time, Oncle César had gone back to the cellar, and from the open trap-door in the pavement came the thumps and scrapes of sacks being moved about below. Jean-Pierre looked down through the trap-door. 'There's a small sack up here we seem to have forgotten!' he called. 'Stand by, and I'll throw it down!' And while Paul-Paul was looking round everywhere on the pavement for the forgotten sack, he suddenly felt himself being lifted into the air, and carried towards the trap-door! And then, with a whoosh and a shout of delight, he found himself sliding fast down the wooden chute into the cellar, where he landed with a bump on the top of a pile of sacks, sending another cloud of white dust flying up into the face of the astonished Oncle César.

'Do that again!' shouted Paul-Paul, trying to scramble back up the slippery chute to the pavement.

'Next Thursday!' called Jean-Pierre. And then, with a loud toot-toot of the lorry's hooter, and a wild flapping up of startled pigeons, he roared away round the square, and was gone.

'Oh, Paul-Paul!' said Marie-Céleste, looking down at him through the trap-door. 'You're covered with flour from head to foot again!'

Paul-Paul smiled up at Marie-Céleste. 'I think Jean-Pierre's super!' he said.

And Marie-Céleste smiled back. 'Yes, so do I,' she said.

CHAPTER 6

A ride in the country

🍀

AFTER this, Paul-Paul always made sure that he was at the Boulangerie on Thursdays, when Jean-Pierre delivered the flour from the mill. He always helped with the unloading of the lorry, and the unloading always ended with Jean-Pierre picking him up and throwing him down the chute into the cellar.

Paul-Paul thought that a week was a very long time to wait for Jean-Pierre's next visit, but he needn't have worried. Soon Jean-Pierre began to call in at the Boulangerie on other days of the week, just to say hallo, if he happened to be passing on one of his delivery rounds. Often, when Paul-Paul was playing football in his school playground between lessons, he could see Jean-Pierre's bright blue lorry parked outside the Boulangerie on the other side of the square. And after school, when Paul-Paul was at the Boulangerie himself, Jean-Pierre would often call in again. They could always tell when he was coming, because of all the squawking of chickens, and barking of dogs, and squealing of tyres, and loud toot-tootings of the lorry's hooter, and wild flapping up of pigeons, which always heralded Jean-Pierre's arrival. Paul-Paul wished that he was old enough to drive a big lorry very fast like that. And he wished that he could go for a ride in the lorry, too.

This second wish soon came true. One afternoon, when Marie-Céleste and Paul-Paul and Jean-Pierre were all sitting in Marie-Céleste's pastry-kitchen, having a cake and a cup of coffee together, Marie-Céleste and Paul-Paul began talking about going for another walk in the forest the next day, which was Saturday.

'I wish I could come too,' said Jean-Pierre. 'But I've got to work.' And then he said, 'I know! Instead of going for a walk, why don't you both come with me on my delivery round?'

Marie-Céleste and Paul-Paul both thought this was a wonderful idea.

'But not if you're going to drive like a maniac!' said Marie-Céleste.

'I'll drive like a snail!' promised Jean-Pierre.

So the next afternoon, straight after lunch, Jean-Pierre came to fetch Marie-Céleste and Paul-Paul at the Boulangerie, and they all climbed into the big blue lorry. There was just room for all three of them in the front, with Paul-Paul squeezed in the middle.

'It's your job to hoot the hooter,' Jean-Pierre said to Paul-Paul. He showed Paul-Paul how to press the big black button in the middle of the steering wheel, and said, 'Every time we go round a corner, or come to a crossroads, or there's something in the way, you give a good loud toot. All right? Now off we go!' And then he pressed the starter, and with a loud bang and a roar the engine started, and off they went.

First they drove all the way round the square, with Paul-Paul giving a good loud toot at each of the four corners. And then they set off down the road to the station, which was at the edge of the village, where the open country began. Paul-Paul hooted at several dogs and cats and chickens, and also at one or two housewives with shopping baskets who crossed the road in front of them. He felt very grand, riding along high up in the big lorry, hooting at everyone.

Soon they arrived at the station, and waited at the level crossing while an express train to Paris went shrieking past. Paul-Paul was very excited. He had been to the station before, to meet Louis-Philippe off the train when he came home on leave, or his aunts and uncles when they came on a visit, but he had never been to the open country beyond the railway line.

At last the shriek of the express train faded away into the distance, the signal changed with a clank, and the two red and white striped poles which had been barring the way across the level crossing slowly lifted into the air. Jean-Pierre started the lorry's engine again, and they drove over the level crossing and into the open country. Soon they were bowling down the long straight road, with lines of poplar trees on either side, and big fields stretching away beyond the poplars. Paul-Paul looked back through the little window behind him, and saw Fleury-des-Bois already looking very small in the distance, nestling at the edge of the forest, which looked like a great green sea. Even while Paul-Paul watched, the village grew smaller and smaller. Jean-Pierre had promised to drive like a snail, but he seemed to be driving like the wind! But Marie-Céleste didn't mind. She was looking out of the window, and smiling happily.

How huge the country was! The great, flat plain stretched away all round them to the distant blue horizon, divided into huge fields by lines so straight that they might have been drawn with a ruler. On and on the fields stretched, some newly ploughed and brown, some green with grass and dotted with grazing cows, but most of them a bluish green with growing corn. Here and there, miles apart from one another, there were farms or villages, looking tiny on the great plain. Paul-Paul felt very proud that he was French, and belonged to such a big country.

After several miles, Jean-Pierre slowed down, and they turned off the main road on to a dusty cart-track leading away across the fields. It was a very narrow, bumpy track, and as they drove on, it grew more and more bumpy.

'Where are we going?' asked Paul-Paul.

'Wait and see!' said Jean-Pierre.

Just then, Paul-Paul saw that the cart-track was leading towards a big group of elms not far ahead. As they drew nearer, he saw that under the elms stood a grey stone house, with several other stone buildings, some large, some small, beside it. And near the buildings were some cows, and some pigs, and a lot of chickens. They were going to a farm!

'I've got some sacks of cattle-food to deliver here,' Jean-Pierre explained. 'I hope you're ready to do some unloading, Paul-Paul!'

At the tops of the elms were lots of rooks' nests. As the lorry approached, all the rooks flapped up into the air, and wheeled round and round above the farm in a great dark cloud, cawing loudly. And then all the cows started mooing, and the pigs grunted, and the chickens ran squawking out of the way, and several dogs started barking. The farmer and his wife, and their children, and several farm-labourers and dairy-maids all came out of the buildings, smiling and waving. 'Bonjour, Jean-Pierre!' they all called out.

'I've got a workman with me today!' said Jean-Pierre, jumping out of the lorry. And he helped Paul-Paul scramble up on to the back of the lorry, and then together, with cries of 'Op-là!' they threw down the sacks of cattle-food to the farmer and his workers in the yard below. Marie-Céleste stood watching and smiling as she talked to the farmer's wife.

When the unloading was finished, Marie-Céleste and Paul-Paul looked round the farm together, while Jean-Pierre went into the farmhouse with the farmer to talk business.

There was a great deal to see. Marie-Céleste and Paul-Paul looked over the walls of the pig-sties, and saw big grey sows lying on their sides, with lots of little pink squealing piglets scrambling about all over them. They looked over the stable-doors of sheds where newly-born calves were being fed from buckets by a young farm-lad. They stood in the doorway of the milking-shed, looking down the long rows of cows cudding contentedly as they were milked, and listening to the soothing, rhythmic sound of the milking-machines: wheeze-plonk! wheeze-plonk! wheeze-plonk! They also looked into the dairy, where the dairy-maids were busy churning butter and making cheese, ready to sell in the market at Fleury-des-Bois. How busy everyone was! And how clean and tidy the farm was! Paul-Paul had always thought that farms would be very muddy. But all the farm-workers wore clean aprons or overalls, and the cobbled yard was newly swept and damp from being washed, and everywhere there was a clean, fresh, breezy smell of disinfectant.

Paul-Paul would have liked to stay on the farm much longer, but Jean-Pierre had lots more deliveries to make. So they climbed back into the lorry, and on they went, back down the long dusty track to the main road, while everyone on the farm stood waving goodbye, and the rooks wheeled round and round above the elms again.

Soon the lorry was bowling along the main road again, and after a few more miles they turned down another bumpy track to another farm, and then on to another, and another, and another. Or sometimes, instead of going to a farm, they stopped at a village, and delivered some sacks of flour to the Boulangerie there. All the villages they visited were very like Fleury-des-Bois. They all had a square with plane-trees and a war memorial in the middle, and a church with a tall tower, and a Mairie, and a school. The houses had grey stone walls and brown tiled roofs and walled gardens full of fruit-trees, just like the houses in Fleury-des-Bois. But none of the cakes in the Boulangerie windows looked nearly as good as Marie-Céleste's, and none of the girls serving behind the counters was as pretty as she was.

'None of the girls we've seen today is a patch on Marie-Céleste!' Paul-Paul said proudly to Jean-Pierre, while they were unloading some sacks of flour outside a village Boulangerie.

'Aren't they?' said Jean-Pierre, with a smile. 'I wouldn't know. I haven't even noticed them.'

After they had been to one or two more farms and villages, Paul-Paul noticed that the back of the lorry, which had been piled high with sacks when they first started out, was now empty.

'What are we going to do now?' Paul-Paul asked, hoping that they weren't going to go back to Fleury-des-Bois already.

'Wait and see!' answered Jean-Pierre, with a smile.

They drove on. From time to time, during their delivery round, they had come quite close to a little silver river which wound its way in loops and curves across the plain, with poplars all along its banks. Once or twice they had crossed it, over little grey stone bridges. But now the road began to run along beside the river all the time. Paul-Paul saw old men and boys fishing from the banks, and brightly-painted barges chugging along in midstream. Paul-Paul wondered more and more where they could be going.

Then suddenly Jean-Pierre pointed ahead, and said, 'Look, Paul-Paul! What do you think that is?'

Not far ahead, there was a big stone building right at the river's edge. It was square and strong, with lots of little windows in it, and it stood on a bend in the river, so that the river seemed to

encircle it like a moat. At first Paul-Paul thought it might be a castle. But then, as they drew closer, he saw that there was a great big wheel against one side of the building, like a steamer's paddle-wheel, half in and half out of the water. There were also some big yellow letters on the wall of the building, and as they drew closer and closer, Paul-Paul saw that they spelt 'MOULIN DUPRÉ'. It was the mill where Jean-Pierre lived!

With a loud toot-toot on the lorry's hooter, they drew up outside the mill, and got out of the lorry. Paul-Paul stood looking up at the great grey building. It looked bigger than ever now that he was close to it, and a great rumbling and clanking of machinery came from inside. The ground outside was covered with white dust, and clouds of it were drifting out of the open windows and filling the air. Workmen, white with dust from head to foot, went in and out of the big dark doorway, carrying big sacks on their shoulders and whistling cheerfully.

After a moment, Monsieur Dupré himself came out of the mill, and shook hands with Marie-Céleste and Paul-Paul. He looked very like Jean-Pierre. He was tall and handsome, and although his hair was grey and his back was bent, his eyes were just as bright and as blue as Jean-Pierre's. 'Would you like to see round the mill?' he asked.

'Yes, please!' said Marie-Céleste and Paul-Paul.

At first, it was so dark inside the mill, after the bright sunlight outside, and so full of billowing clouds of dust, and so noisy with the rumbling and clanking of machinery, that Paul-Paul couldn't make out anything at all. But soon he got used to the noise and the darkness and the dust, and then he could see enormous piles of sacks waiting to be loaded on to the lorry, and great gleaming metal machines, and mountains of flour and corn. He also saw long ladders going up through little trap-doors to the floor above, and long, gleaming wooden chutes coming down. Now and then streams of corn or flour came rushing down the chutes with a whoosh.

'Goodness, what a lot of different things are happening at once!' said Marie-Céleste. 'It would take me a long time to under-stand it all!'

'I'll explain it all to you from the beginning,' said Jean-Pierre. 'We'll start at the top floor. Come on!'

And while Monsieur Dupré stayed on the ground floor, supervising the work, Jean-Pierre led Marie-Céleste and Paul-Paul up one long ladder after another until they reached the top floor.

Up there it was quiet, and there was no dust. The sun streamed in through the little windows, and the strong oak floor was cleanly swept. There were several piles of different kinds of corn, divided from one another by wooden partitions. Some were bright gold, some pale gold, some white, and some grey, and they all gleamed softly in the shadows.

'Here, come and look out of the window,' said Jean-Pierre.

Marie-Céleste and Paul-Paul looked out of the window at the miles and miles of flat plain, all bluish green with growing corn to the skyline. What a lot of corn there was growing!

'In the autumn, after the harvest,' explained Jean-Pierre, 'we buy all the corn that you can see growing, and keep it up here. And then we turn some of it into cattle-food, and sell it back to the farmers, and some of it into flour and oatmeal, which we sell to the bakers in the villages.'

Then Jean-Pierre showed Marie-Céleste and Paul-Paul each of the different kinds of corn. The bright gold corn was called maize, the pale gold corn was called wheat, the grey corn was called barley, and the white corn was called oats. The more Paul-Paul looked at the piles of corn, the more beautiful they seemed to him.

'Can I touch some?' he asked.

'Of course!' said Jean-Pierre.

Paul-Paul picked up handfuls of each of the different kinds of corn, and let the cool, satiny grains trickle through his fingers. 'It's just like treasure!' he said.

'It *is* treasure,' said Jean-Pierre. 'Every slice of bread you've ever eaten has come from here. Without this corn, we would all die!'

Paul-Paul thought of the farmers ploughing their big fields and growing the corn, and Monsieur Dupré and Jean-Pierre turning the corn into flour in their mill, and Oncle César working in his cellar, turning the flour into bread. What important jobs they all had! Paul-Paul sighed deeply, and hoped that he would do something as useful as that when he was grown-up.

'Come on!' said Jean-Pierre. 'Now I'll show you how we turn the corn into flour and oatmeal and cattle-food.'

On the next floor down Jean-Pierre showed them how the machines worked. Marie-Céleste and Paul-Paul saw workmen pouring the corn into the tops of the great rumbling, clanking, quivering machines, and then they saw the corn coming out at the bottom, looking quite different. The hard, round, bright gold grains of maize came out as corn-flakes, and the feathery grey barley came out looking like little silver pearls. The pale gold wheat came out as fine white flour, and the oats came out as oatmeal, or soft grey porridge oats. It all seemed quite miraculous to Paul-Paul.

After they had finished looking at the machines, they went back to the ground floor.

'Well, what do you think of our mill?' asked Monsieur Dupré.

'It's beautiful!' said Paul-Paul.

'It's very different from when I was your age,' said Monsieur Dupré. 'When my grandfather was the miller, they still used the old mill-wheel. There was none of this modern machinery then.'

'Can we see the mill-wheel?' asked Marie-Céleste.

'Of course!' said Monsieur Dupré. And they all went out through a little door in the side of the mill, and found themselves standing beside the great mill-wheel, with the river racing past just at their feet.

'The river runs very fast round this bend,' explained Monsieur Dupré. 'That's why the mill was built just here, hundreds of years ago, when they had to have water to turn the wheel and grind the corn, instead of modern machinery.'

Paul-Paul looked at the great wheel. Its big, heavy spokes, and its cogs and axles, were rusty, and its paddles were draped with thick green water-weed. 'Doesn't it work any more?' he asked sadly.

'It might,' said Monsieur Dupré. 'Jean-Pierre used to tinker with it a lot, before he went into the Army.'

Jean-Pierre took hold of a great rusty lever beside the mill-wheel, and began to push it. It was so big and rusty that it took all his strength to move it, but at last, with a shriek and a clank, it moved. And then, after a moment, there came a great groan from the mill-wheel, and very slowly it began to turn. The racing river splashed and bubbled against the paddles, and little by little the mill-wheel began to turn faster. Its big paddles went splash! splash! splash! into the water one after another as it went round.

Groan . . . creak . . . splash! Groan . . . creak . . . splash went the great mill-wheel, turning just as it had for hundreds and hundreds of years in the olden days, grinding the corn into flour so that people would always have bread to eat. Paul-Paul could have watched it turning for a long time, and he could see that Marie-Céleste felt just the same.

But Monsieur Dupré said, 'What about some tea?' And he led them over a little bridge to a house on the other side of the river. It was a beautiful house, and it looked very old. It had a wide, velvety lawn sloping down to the river, with weeping willows overhanging the margin, and a little wooden landing-stage with an old punt tied up to it.

Jean-Pierre's mother was waiting for them, with a special tea all laid out on a table on the lawn under the trees. She was nearly as pretty as Marie-Céleste, Paul-Paul thought, and she gave them a very welcoming smile.

While they were having tea, Paul-Paul kept looking all round at the lovely old house, and the velvety lawn, and the silver river flowing round the garden in a great curve. There were fruit-trees in the garden, and their pink and white blossom was beginning to fall, scattering the lawn and the garden table with petals. Across the river, the mill-wheel was still turning, its groan . . . creak . . . splash! Groan . . . creak . . . splash turned into a soothing murmur by distance. Paul-Paul thought it was the most beautiful place he had ever seen. And he could see that Marie-Céleste felt just the same about it. For a long time she was very quiet and dreamy, looking round at everything, and listening to the sound of the mill-wheel. And then she smiled at Madame Dupré, and said, 'What a perfect place to live! How lucky you are!'

At this, Monsieur and Madame Dupré and Jean-Pierre all suddenly looked very happy. Paul-Paul could see that they were trying to hide how pleased they were.

'Well, it will all belong to Jean-Pierre one day!' said Monsieur Dupré. 'To him, and his wife, and his children! And now I must get back to work!' And he went back over the bridge to the mill, smiling to himself all the way.

Soon after this, Jean-Pierre drove Marie-Céleste and Paul-Paul back to Fleury-des-Bois. On the way home, Paul-Paul kept thinking about the special way everyone had looked, and what Monsieur Dupré had said just before he went back to the mill. Everyone was behaving as if there was a secret, but Paul-Paul had already guessed what it was!

CHAPTER 7

A happy day for Fleury-des-Bois

❧

A FEW days later the secret was out. Jean-Pierre and Marie-Céleste were going to get married.

Everyone in Fleury-des-Bois was delighted. It was spring, and what could be better than a nice wedding to look forward to? In the next few weeks, while all the preparations were being made, everyone seemed to be in the best of spirits. The tradesmen and shopkeepers whistled as they went about their work, and the housewives sang like larks as they flapped their dusters from their upstairs windows. Even Monsieur le Maire and Monsieur l'Abbé were the same. Monsieur le Maire stood on the steps of the Mairie and smiled to himself as he looked at his gold watch. 'Bang on time!' he said to Paul-Paul cheerfully, as Paul-Paul went by, and the church clock chimed the hour. And Monsieur l'Abbé stood on the church steps, smiling to himself as he looked up at the sky. 'Look, Paul-Paul!' he said gaily, as Paul-Paul went by, pointing up at the falling fruit-tree blossom petals, which the breeze was whirling about in clouds above the rooftops. 'Just like confetti from Heaven!'

No one was more delighted at the news than Paul-Paul. It had already been decided that Marie-Céleste and Jean-Pierre were going to live in the beautiful old house by the mill as soon as they were married, and that Paul-Paul was going to go and stay with them sometimes. He was going to help Jean-Pierre at the mill, and Jean-Pierre was also going to teach him to swim, and fish, and punt.

The only person who wasn't pleased about the wedding was Mademoiselle Augustine. 'Hm!' she sniffed. 'That Jean-Pierre Dupré is a no-good scallywag and a tearaway, and he always has been! Look at the way he drives! He'll never settle, and it'll all come to no good.'

'Nonsense!' everyone said. 'He's just high-spirited, that's all. He'll soon quieten down when he's married.'

'Ha! I'll believe that when I see it!' snorted Mademoiselle Augustine, and she went back into her house and banged the door.

'Silly old sour-puss!' everyone said. 'She's just jealous, because she never got married herself!' And they thought no more about it.

Meanwhile, Marie-Céleste and Jean-Pierre were both very busy getting ready for the wedding.

Marie-Céleste was making her wedding dress, with its veil and its long train. Paul-Paul loved to watch her sewing all the yards and yards of beautiful white lace with tiny stitches, while he held the pins for her. Her needle flashed in and out so fast, the dress and the long train seemed to grow under her fingers, and she sang happily as she sewed. The lace for the dress had a pattern of white leaves and flowers, and that was beautiful enough. But the lace for the long train was even better. As well as leaves and branches and flowers in its pattern, there were castles, and princes and princesses, and knights, and deer, and unicorns, all as white as snow. The lace was so perfectly white that Paul-Paul wasn't allowed to touch it until Marie-Céleste had made sure that his hands were clean. And Jean-Pierre wasn't even allowed to see it until Marie-Céleste came down the aisle of the church wearing it on their wedding day.

As well as her wedding dress, Marie-Céleste was also making a page-boy suit for Paul-Paul, for he was going to be her page-boy at the wedding. There were not going to be any bridesmaids. There was only going to be Paul-Paul, carrying Marie-Céleste's long train up the aisle of the church all by himself.

Paul-Paul had already tried his page-boy suit on. It was made of blue velvet, with a white lace collar and white lace cuffs. When Paul-Paul looked at himself in the mirror, he thought he looked just like a page-boy from the olden days. He looked just like the

page-boy in his unicorn picture, which was how he had always
wanted to look.

As well as making her wedding dress and Paul-Paul's page-boy
suit, Marie-Céleste would soon have to start making her wedding
cake too, and icing it, so that she was very busy indeed.

Jean-Pierre was just as busy, working extra hard at the mill, to
earn the money to take Marie-Céleste away for their honeymoon.
He was also getting the house ready for them to live in it.
Monsieur and Madame Dupré had already gone to live in another
house a little further up the river. Jean-Pierre was giving everything in the house a new coat of paint, or a new covering of wallpaper. Marie-Céleste went out to the mill-house to help him in her
spare time, and sometimes Paul-Paul went too. All the time they
were there, they could hear the groan . . . creak . . . splash!
Groan . . . creak . . . splash of the mill-wheel still turning on the
other side of the river. Jean-Pierre had promised Marie-Céleste
that he would always keep it turning from now on.

Jean-Pierre was also very busy learning all about the running of
the mill. Monsieur Dupré was going to retire as soon as Jean-
Pierre and Marie-Céleste were back from their honeymoon, and
then Jean-Pierre would be running the mill by himself.

'And a fine miller he'll be!' said Monsieur Dupré, slapping
Jean-Pierre on the back. 'He's a hard worker, and very clever with
machinery. He's full of ideas about how to make the machines
work faster, and grind twice as much corn in half the time.
Nothing ever goes fast enough for Jean-Pierre!'

It was true that Jean-Pierre still hadn't changed at all, although
he was getting married so soon, and everyone had said that marriage would quieten him down. He still drove his lorry at
breakneck speed, and he was still as gay and as energetic and as
full of fun and adventure as ever. But Paul-Paul liked him like
that, and hoped he would never change.

Mademoiselle Augustine was still prophesying doom, but no
one took any notice of her. Paul-Paul was sure that she was wrong,
and that everything would have turned out perfectly, if it hadn't
been for Jean-Pierre's friend, Alphonse Duval.

CHAPTER 8

Alphonse

❧

EVER since Paul-Paul had first met Jean-Pierre, he had always heard a lot about Alphonse. First of all, in church on Easter Sunday, he had heard Mademoiselle Augustine whispering that Jean-Pierre and Alphonse had been the two naughtiest boys in Fleury-des-Bois when they were younger. And then, whenever Jean-Pierre had told Paul-Paul stories about when he was a little boy, they had always been about the naughty things he and Alphonse had done together. From Jean-Pierre's stories, it sounded as if all the worst things they had done had been Alphonse's idea. It sounded as if Alphonse had been ten times naughtier than Jean-Pierre himself.

All this had made Paul-Paul long to meet Alphonse. But Alphonse was away in the Army. He had gone into the Army at the same time as Jean-Pierre, and he hadn't come out yet.

'But he's coming home soon,' Jean-Pierre had promised, 'and then you'll meet him.'

Sometimes, though, Paul-Paul wasn't quite sure if he was going to like Alphonse when he met him. From some of the stories Jean-Pierre told, when they were sitting in Marie-Céleste's pastry-kitchen, he thought Alphonse sounded a bit mean. Once, for instance, Jean-Pierre described how Alphonse had had the idea of making stink-bombs and throwing them over people's garden walls. So Alphonse had made the stink-bombs, and Jean-Pierre had thrown them into people's gardens; and Jean-Pierre had got caught, and had been punished.

'And then did Alphonse own up too, and share your punishment?' Paul-Paul asked.

'Not him!' said Jean-Pierre, laughing.

'How rotten of him!' said Marie-Céleste, banging down her mixing bowl. 'He doesn't sound at all like a good friend to me. In nearly all the stories you've told, Alphonse seems to have talked you into doing something naughty, and then left you to take all the punishment!'

Paul-Paul had been thinking that too. But Jean-Pierre said, 'He was a wizard at making stink-bombs, and fireworks, and booby-traps, though!' as if this made up for Alphonse's meanness. Paul-Paul thought that Alphonse must be all right if Jean-Pierre still liked him so much. And he did love hearing about all their adventures.

Paul-Paul especially loved hearing about all the exciting things Jean-Pierre and Alphonse had done together in the Army. They had been to lots of foreign countries, and had ridden in tanks, and worn camouflage, and fired big guns. But as well as all this, Jean-Pierre explained, they had each had a special job as well. Alphonse had been a mechanic, and Jean-Pierre had been a dispatch rider. Alphonse had to see that all the motorbikes and jeeps and tanks were working properly, and Jean-Pierre had to carry urgent messages to the General on a very fast motorbike. The messages were so urgent, and the motorbikes so fast and powerful, that lots of Army dispatch riders crashed and got killed.

'Weren't you scared?' asked Paul-Paul.

'No, it was marvellous!' said Jean-Pierre, his eyes shining at the memory. 'Tearing along on a powerful Army motorbike at more than a hundred miles an hour! – I felt like the king of the world! No motorbike could go too fast for me! Alphonse used to tinker about with mine to make it go even faster. He's a wizard with engines. We used to take the bike and go motor-racing with it whenever we had the chance.'

'And did you win?' asked Paul-Paul.

'Of course!' said Jean-Pierre. 'Alphonse wanted me to leave the Army and become a professional racing driver, and he would have been my mechanic. He was furious when I came home to run the mill instead. I don't know what he'll say when he finds I'm getting married. Still,' he added, his eyes beginning to shine with excitement again, 'there's no reason why we shouldn't save up for a bike, and still go racing sometimes.'

'Isn't there?' cried Marie-Céleste, banging down her mixing bowl again. Paul-Paul had noticed that she was growing paler and paler while Jean-Pierre was talking. 'Oh yes there jolly well is!' she said. 'You've got me to think of now. And soon enough you'll have children to think of too. You're not leaving me with a family of orphans to bring up all by myself!'

'But – ' began Jean-Pierre.

'No buts!' cried Marie-Céleste. 'You're to promise you'll never go racing again! Otherwise I shall just marry someone more sensible!'

'All right then, marry someone more sensible!' shouted Jean-Pierre angrily. And for a moment he glared at Marie-Céleste, who stood facing him with her cheeks flushed and her grey eyes flashing. She looked more beautiful than ever, Paul-Paul thought, and he could see that Jean-Pierre couldn't help thinking so too. And then at last Jean-Pierre said, in a dignified voice, 'Very well then, since you insist, I promise.'

'And you can tell your horrible friend Alphonse that, when you see him!' cried Marie-Céleste.

'And I'll tell my horrible friend Alphonse that, when I see him,' said Jean-Pierre soothingly. And at this, both he and Marie-Céleste started laughing.

'Ah, who wants silly old Alphonse, and silly old motor-racing,' said Jean-Pierre gaily, putting his arm round Marie-Céleste and giving her a kiss, 'when I've got you, and the mill?'

Paul-Paul was sure that Jean-Pierre really meant it. And then Alphonse came home.

Alphonse came back to Fleury-des-Bois soon after Jean-Pierre and Marie-Céleste had announced their engagement, and got a job at a petrol station on the main road between Fleury-des-Bois and the mill. Marie-Céleste and Paul-Paul soon met him, when they were on their way to the mill with Jean-Pierre one Saturday afternoon to do some decorating, and they stopped to buy petrol.

Right up to the moment when Paul-Paul first saw Alphonse, he still wasn't sure if he was going to like him or not. Marie-Céleste seemed to have made up her mind that she wasn't, but then she was a girl, and probably couldn't understand that some-one could be nice just because he was a wizard with stink-bombs and motorbikes. Paul-Paul thought that he probably would like Alphonse, and he felt very excited as they pulled up at the petrol station.

But as soon as Paul-Paul saw Alphonse standing by the petrol pumps, an awful doubt crept over him. First of all, Alphonse was ugly. He was very big and burly, and he had thick, black, tangly, greasy hair, and his overalls were black with oil and dirt. And then he was very rude, Paul-Paul thought. There was a nasty mocking look in his bold black eyes as he watched the lorry pull up at the petrol station, and he didn't even say hallo to Marie-Céleste and Paul-Paul. He just stood there and laughed.

'Quite the family man already, aren't we?' he said jeeringly to Jean-Pierre, as Jean-Pierre jumped out of the lorry. 'I never thought to see *you* driving along like an old lady!'

Paul-Paul thought this was a horrid thing to say. But Jean-Pierre just laughed, and slapped Alphonse on the back. It didn't seem as if anything Alphonse said could annoy him.

After this, whenever they stopped there for petrol, Alphonse was always very rude. But Jean-Pierre never seemed to mind, and he often spent a long time talking to Alphonse about engines. Sometimes the two of them tinkered with the lorry's engine for what seemed like hours. Every time they stopped at the petrol station, Marie-Céleste looked more annoyed, but Jean-Pierre never even seemed to notice.

One day, only a very short time before the wedding, when they stopped at the petrol station, Alphonse said to Jean-Pierre, 'Here! I've got something to show you!' And from behind the petrol pumps he wheeled out a big, shiny, powerful-looking motorbike. Jean-Pierre gave a low whistle of admiration. 'A chap brought it in for repairs,' said Alphonse. 'I've mended it now, and it goes like a bomb. Do you want to try it?'

'Do I?' cried Jean-Pierre, leaping into the saddle of the motorbike. 'What a question!' And he kicked a pedal, and with a great ear-splitting roar the powerful engine started.

'Jean-Pierre! No!' cried Marie-Céleste.

But it was too late. Jean-Pierre didn't even hear her above the thundering roar of the motorbike's engine, and his blue eyes were so bright with excitement that he hardly seemed to see her either. And then, with an even louder roar from the motorbike, he swept round the petrol station in a great cloud of dust, and was gone, away down the long, straight poplar-lined road, and out of sight, going like a bullet.

'Ha! That's more like my old pal Jean-Pierre!' said Alphonse with a grin, standing with his oily arms folded as he watched Jean-Pierre vanish over the horizon. 'A hundred miles an hour at the very least! That's what I like to see!'

'And I'd like to see you swinging from the end of a rope!' said Marie-Céleste furiously, jumping out of the lorry and going up to Alphonse. 'If Jean-Pierre has a crash and gets killed, you'll be nothing better than a murderer.'

'He'd be better off dead than spending the rest of his life rotting at that boring old mill with you!' shouted Alphonse. 'He ought to be a racing driver!'

'If you think being a racing driver is so marvellous, why don't you become one yourself?' Marie-Céleste shouted back scornfully. 'But you're too scared, aren't you? You want to have all the excitement while Jean-Pierre takes all the risks, the same as you always have! You're nothing but a coward and a parasite!'

'And you're a silly old cow!' shouted Alphonse, turning quite purple with rage.

At this, Marie-Céleste laughed in his face, and then turned her back on him and came back to the lorry. She looked very pleased with herself. 'Good for you, Marie-Céleste!' whispered Paul-Paul, who had been wishing he was big enough to punch Alphonse on the nose.

All this time, Paul-Paul's heart had been beating painfully fast. He wished he could punch Alphonse on the nose, but at the same time he wished he was tearing along on that motorbike with

3

Jean-Pierre. And now that Marie-Céleste was standing beside the lorry, pale with worry as she gazed up the road, Paul-Paul began to feel worried too. Jean-Pierre had been out of sight for a long time. Perhaps he was lying in the road a few miles away in a pool of blood!

And then suddenly Paul-Paul shouted, 'There he is!' For on the horizon he could see a tiny white cloud of dust. And sure enough, as he and Marie-Céleste watched with sighs of relief, it grew bigger and bigger and noisier and noisier as it came very fast down the road towards them. And then, with a great thundering roar, Jean-Pierre was sweeping round the petrol station again in a wide curve, waving at them and smiling. But instead of stopping, he began to drive round and round the petrol station in circles. Round and round he roared, very fast – round the petrol pumps, round the lorry, and round Alphonse, who grinned and shouted, 'Atta boy! That's the stuff! Faster!' At this, Jean-Pierre smiled back and went faster still, tearing round in smaller and smaller loops and circles until he was missing things by inches, tearing at breakneck speed through narrow gaps, then using his foot on the ground to spin the motorbike right round in a swirl of dust, and roaring round again. His blue eyes were faraway and shining, as if he was under a spell, the dust was whirling after him in a great white plume, and the motorbike seemed to be rearing and prancing as he rode it.

'Oh, Marie-Céleste, he looks just like a circus pony!' shouted Paul-Paul. 'He looks just like a *unicorn!*'

Very pale, Marie-Céleste nodded, and gave a funny, sad little smile. 'Yes,' she agreed. 'Just like a unicorn.'

At last Jean-Pierre stopped, and made the motorbike's engine go quieter. 'How was that?' he asked, with a smile.

Paul-Paul cheered and clapped, but Alphonse only shrugged, and said, 'Not bad. I've seen better.'

At this, Jean-Pierre's eyes flashed, and he looked as if he was going to go roaring round faster than ever. But Marie-Céleste said quickly, 'Jean-Pierre, it was marvellous. You're terribly good at it. But please stop now. It's just as dangerous as racing, and you did promise.'

'Stop?' cried Jean-Pierre, with a laugh. 'But that would be selfish! I haven't given anyone a ride yet. Who wants a ride?'

Paul-Paul was out of the lorry, and clambering on to the back of the motorbike before Marie-Céleste could stop him.

'No, Paul-Paul!' cried Marie-Céleste, going paler than ever. 'Jean-Pierre, you must be mad!'

'Oh, don't worry,' said Jean-Pierre cheerfully. 'I won't take him far, and I'll drive very slowly. Put your arms right round me, Paul-Paul, and hold on tight!'

Paul-Paul did as Jean-Pierre told him. And then the roar of the engine grew very loud again, and the motorbike seemed to lift under them like a great bird. Round the petrol station it carried them in a wide curve, past Alphonse, grinning more than ever by the petrol pumps, past Marie-Céleste, leaning against the lorry and looking quite ill, and then away up the long straight road.

Jean-Pierre had said he would drive slowly, but to Paul-Paul they seemed to be going wonderfully fast – much faster than they had ever gone in the lorry. The wind rushed past their faces, and the road flew past beneath them, and the poplars flashed past like lightning on either side. And all the time there was the powerful thundering of the engine in their ears. It was the most exciting feeling Paul-Paul had ever had in his life. It was like listening to the big drum in the village band, and sliding down a very long chute, all rolled into one! It was just like riding a unicorn!

'All right, Paul-Paul?' shouted Jean-Pierre, over his shoulder.

'Yes!' shouted Paul-Paul. 'Go faster!'

And Jean-Pierre laughed, and went faster.

The faster they went, the faster Paul-Paul wanted to go. But after a while, although he still loved it, he found that the thunder of the engine, and the wind in his face, were making him strangely sleepy. So he stopped looking at the road over Jean-Pierre's shoulder, and leaned his head against Jean-Pierre's back instead, and closed his eyes. It was warmer like that, and not quite so noisy. And with his eyes closed, it was more than ever like sliding down a long, dark chute; more than ever like galloping through the wildest depths of the forest on a unicorn's back, with his arms clasped tightly round its strong white neck, and the sound of its hoofs drumming in his ears . . .

'Tuwit-tuwoo!' a rather shaky voice said suddenly. 'Wake up, Paul-Paul!'

Paul-Paul opened his eyes and sat up with a jerk. They were back at the petrol station! The motorbike's engine had stopped, and the silence made Paul-Paul's ears sing. He smiled and rubbed his eyes as Marie-Céleste lifted him off the motorbike. 'I thought I was riding a unicorn,' he said. 'It was lovely!'

But Marie-Céleste didn't smile back. 'You were asleep,' she said. And then she gave Jean-Pierre a long, strange look. 'You realize, don't you,' she said, 'that in another moment he'd have fallen off?'

Jean-Pierre went pale and quiet. Then he got off the motorbike and handed it to Alphonse. 'Here, take the bloody thing!' he said.

At this, Alphonse's face went dark with anger again. 'I'll make a racing driver of you yet, if it kills me!' he shouted after Jean-Pierre, as Jean-Pierre climbed into the lorry with Marie-Céleste and Paul-Paul.

'Oh, come off it!' said Jean-Pierre, as he started the lorry's engine.

Then Alphonse's face suddenly changed, and he said in a friendly voice, 'But you'll still come with me to watch the motor-racing next Saturday, like you promised, won't you?'

'I doubt it,' said Jean-Pierre, with an uneasy glance at Marie-Céleste, 'but I'll see.'

And then they drove away from the petrol station towards the mill. And when Paul-Paul looked back through the little window behind them, he saw that Alphonse was grinning again as he watched them go.

CHAPTER 9

A very sad day
for Fleury-des-Bois

♣

NEXT Saturday, Jean-Pierre did go to the motor-racing with
Alphonse after all. Marie-Céleste didn't want him to go, but Jean-
Pierre said, 'It's the very last time I'll ever go, and I did promise
Alphonse.' And as he wasn't going to drive in the race, but only
watch it, Marie-Céleste couldn't very well object.

'And after all,' she said to Paul-Paul, 'I must let him have his
last fling before he gets married!'

The motor-race that Saturday was in a town not far from
Fleury-des-Bois, and it was one of the biggest and most important
races in the whole of France. Several other young men from the
village were going to watch it. Louis-Philippe, who had come
home on leave especially for Marie-Céleste's wedding, was going
with some of his friends. Paul-Paul asked his mother if he could
go too.

'Certainly not!' said his mother. 'With all those fast cars and
motorbikes, and all those rough men and those crowds, and all
the noise and the excitement and the accidents, you'd be sure to
get lost, or trampled underfoot, or run over!'

So Paul-Paul spent the afternoon helping Marie-Céleste sew
her wedding-dress, and having another fitting for his page-boy
suit.

Jean-Pierre and Alphonse and all the other young men from the
village had gone to the motor-racing by train, and when it was
time for them all to come home again, Marie-Céleste and Paul-Paul
decided to walk down to the station to meet them.

When the train came in, Louis-Philippe and his friends, and all the other young men from the village, leapt out, talking and shouting excitedly. But although Marie-Céleste and Paul-Paul waited and waited, and looked eagerly at everyone who got out of the train, there was no sign of either Jean-Pierre or Alphonse. And then the train doors slammed shut, the whistle blew, the train pulled out of the station, and the platform was empty.

Louis-Philippe and his friends were just leaving the station, still chattering together excitedly. 'Louis-Philippe!' Marie-Céleste and Paul-Paul called after him. 'Where are Jean-Pierre and Alphonse? Why haven't they come home with you?'

Louis-Philippe had been talking so excitedly with his friends that he hadn't noticed Marie-Céleste and Paul-Paul waiting on the platform. Now that he did, his face, which was already pink with excitement, suddenly went very red. 'Er, um,' he said, looking at his feet. There seemed to be something he didn't want to tell them.

'Oh my God, what's happened?' cried Marie-Céleste, turning very pale. 'Don't tell me there's been an accident!'

'No, no, nothing like that,' said Louis-Philippe, very reassuringly, but he was still red in the face, and he looked longingly after his friends. 'There was just this super fast motorbike for sale at the race-track, and, um, Jean-Pierre bought it.'

'Bought it?' cried Marie-Céleste in amazement. 'But it must have cost more than a hundred pounds. Where on earth did he get the money?'

At this, Louis-Philippe pulled unhappily at the moustache he was trying to grow, and stared down at his feet.

'Are you telling me that he bought it with the money for our honeymoon?' asked Marie-Céleste, her eyes beginning to flash with anger. 'I'll kill him when I see him!'

'No, no!' said Louis-Philippe. 'I mean, yes, yes, but don't worry! He said he was going to sell the bike again straight away after the race, so nothing's lost. And besides, there was a lot of prize money,' he added, looking more cheerful, 'so you'll have a better honeymoon than ever!'

'What do you mean, after the race?' shrieked Marie-Céleste. 'What prize-money?'

'Jean-Pierre went in for the race,' said Louis-Philippe, looking all excited again at the memory. 'The big race! And he won it! It was marvellous! There were lots of crashes, but Jean-Pierre overtook everyone, and won! The crowd went mad! They carried him to the prize-giving stand on their shoulders! Everyone said he was the fastest and most daring driver they had ever seen, and that he could easily become the champion of France! Our Jean-Pierre Dupré, of Fleury-des-Bois! You ought to be proud of him!'

'Whoopee!' shouted Paul-Paul.

But Marie-Céleste was ominously silent. Louis-Philippe went very red again, and so did Paul-Paul.

'And when does he say he's coming home?' asked Marie-Céleste.

'Tonight, of course,' said Louis-Philippe. 'He's only staying to sell the motorbike, and celebrate a bit with Alphonse and the other drivers. He'll be home on the last train tonight, so don't worry!' And with that he turned and ran up the road after his friends.

Marie-Céleste and Paul-Paul left the station and walked slowly back to the village. Marie-Céleste didn't say anything for a while, and neither did Paul-Paul.

Then at last Paul-Paul said sadly, 'Jean-Pierre broke his promise.'

'Yes, but can't you imagine what happened?' Marie-Céleste burst out bitterly. 'Alphonse must have persuaded him just to try the motorbike out a little. And once Jean-Pierre's on a motorbike, he turns into a different person and forgets about everything except going faster and faster. You could see that last Saturday, at the petrol station. And of course Alphonse knew that would happen. He must have planned the whole thing from start to finish.'

She looked so worried and unhappy that Paul-Paul took her hand. 'Never mind, Marie-Céleste!' he said. 'It was only his last fling, and now he's selling the motorbike again. He'll be home tonight, so don't worry.'

'Yes, of course,' said Marie-Céleste, and she squeezed Paul-Paul's hand and tried to smile. And Paul-Paul wondered why she still went on looking so pale and unhappy.

But Jean-Pierre didn't come back later that night. He didn't come back the next day either, which was Sunday, and neither did Alphonse. Everyone thought they must have decided to spend the rest of the weekend at the race-track, tinkering with engines.

'Jean-Pierre oughtn't to have stayed away for the whole week-end without telling anyone,' they said, 'especially when he's getting married so soon. Still, he must have his last fling, and he's sure to be home tomorrow!'

Marie-Céleste and her parents came to Sunday lunch with Paul-Paul's family that day, as they sometimes did. Everyone was being very cheerful and pretending nothing was wrong. But Marie-Céleste looked sick with worry, and hardly ate anything.

The next day was Monday, and everyone went back to work after the weekend. But there was no sign of Alphonse at the petrol station, and no sign of Jean-Pierre at the mill. They still hadn't come home.

Then everyone in Fleury-des-Bois grew very worried. They thought Jean-Pierre and Alphonse might have had an accident. Monsieur Dupré even went to the police station to ask if there was any news, but there wasn't. Then he went to the big town where the motor-race had been, and searched for Jean-Pierre and Alphonse there. But the racing had finished, and all the racing-drivers and mechanics had gone, and there was no sign of Jean-Pierre and Alphonse. Monsieur Dupré came back with his shoulders bent, and his handsome face worn and grey. 'Our only son!' he said. 'How could he do this?'

A whole week passed, and still there was no sign of Jean-Pierre or Alphonse.

'Jean-Pierre's ashamed to come home, because he broke his promise,' some people said. And others said, 'It's that wicked Alphonse. He always *was* a bad influence on Jean-Pierre!' And they added, 'We'll box their ears, both of them, when they come home this weekend!'

Everyone was sure that Jean-Pierre and Alphonse would come

home that weekend. It was the last weekend before the wedding.

But the weekend came, and still there was no sign of them. Instead, when everyone opened their Sunday newspaper, what should they see but a big photograph of Jean-Pierre, wearing a racing-driver's helmet and holding a big silver cup, while beside him stood Alphonse, as dirty and oily as ever, with a grin of triumph on his face. Underneath the photograph were the words: 'Jean-Pierre Dupré, the brilliant and daring new racing driver, with his manager and mechanic, Alphonse Duval.' And then the newspaper went on to say that Jean-Pierre had just won another race that weekend, in a big town on the other side of France. And the weekend after that, he would be racing in a big town in Italy. 'I am arranging for Jean-Pierre Dupré to drive in all the big races in Europe from now on,' Alphonse had told the newspaper man. 'He will soon be a great champion!'

When everyone had read this, they put down their newspapers and stared at each other in a horrified silence. Jean-Pierre hadn't sold the motorbike after all. He had run away to become a racing driver. Worst of all, the day that he was planning to drive in the big race in Italy was his wedding day. He wasn't going to marry Marie-Céleste after all!

'It can't be true!' everyone said. 'Jean-Pierre's always been high-spirited and adventurous, but he's never been really bad and unkind. He'll come to his senses, and be home in time for the wedding.'

Paul-Paul ran all the way to the Boulangerie as soon as he had read the news in the paper. Marie-Céleste was in her pastry-kitchen. She was sitting at the table, looking very faint, and there was a newspaper on the floor at her feet, where she had dropped it.

'He *will* come back in time for the wedding, Marie-Céleste!' cried Paul-Paul. 'He will! He will!'

Marie-Céleste lifted her grey eyes hopelessly to his. 'Wish for it, Paul-Paul,' she said. 'Wish with all your might.'

So Paul-Paul wished. All that week he wished and wished. And he could see that everyone else in Fleury-des-Bois was wishing and hoping too. Every time a train came into the station, everyone looked expectant; but Jean-Pierre was never on it. And every time there was the sound of a lorry coming towards the square, everyone looked up with an eager smile. And then their faces fell again when they saw that it wasn't Jean-Pierre.

The last days went quickly by. Soon there were only three days left; then two; and then it was the very last day before the wedding. And still Jean-Pierre hadn't come back.

That night, Paul-Paul lay awake for a very long time, gazing at his unicorn picture by the glow of his night-light. 'Come back, Jean-Pierre!' he whispered again and again. 'Come back! Oh, please come back!'

But Jean-Pierre didn't come back.

Paul-Paul went to the village square early the next morning. He had hoped to see the fairy-lights strung up in the plane-trees, and the band lined up on the steps of the Mairie, ready for the wedding. But there were no decorations, and the square was empty. It started to drizzle, and the pigeons sat huddled in rows on the ledges of the war memorial, with their feathers fluffed out and their heads tucked under their wings. The blinds of the Boulangerie were drawn. Paul-Paul didn't like to go and knock on the door, but he didn't want to go away either, so he just went on standing in the middle of the square.

After a while, one or two people came to the square to see if there was any news, and then several more people came. Soon there were quite a lot of people standing about under the shelter of the plane-trees, talking in quiet, sad voices. 'What a terrible shame!' they murmured. 'What a very sad day for Fleury-des-Bois!' And then, one by one, they shrugged, and said, 'Still, there it is!' and went home.

Soon Paul-Paul was alone in the square again. And then at last he could bear it no longer, and he ran across to the Boulangerie and knocked on the door. No one answered. 'It's me! It's Paul-Paul!' he called, knocking again.

At last the door opened, and Marie-Céleste let him in. It was strangely dark in the Boulangerie with the blinds drawn, and Paul-Paul could hardly see Marie-Céleste's face. For a moment they stood there in silence.

'Well, that's that, Paul-Paul!' said Marie-Céleste, trying to sound brave and sensible.

At this, Paul-Paul couldn't help giving a sob. 'Oh don't, Paul-Paul!' said Marie-Céleste, and she gave a sob too. And then they put their arms round each other, and cried and cried.

CHAPTER 10

A real friend

♣

FOR a long time after this, life was very hard for Marie-Céleste and Paul-Paul. Marie-Céleste never smiled or sang as she worked in the Boulangerie now, and often she was too sad even to talk to Paul-Paul while he was helping her.

'You run off and play with the other children,' she said to him sometimes, when she was feeling especially bad. 'It's no fun for you here with me.'

'It's all right, Marie-Céleste,' Paul-Paul would say with a cheerful smile, going on stirring the cake-mix energetically. In fact, he often did rather long to go off and play with the other children instead, but he knew how lonely Marie-Céleste felt. And he hadn't forgotten how she had come to see him every day of her holidays when he was ill in bed.

The worst days were Thursdays, when a strange workman delivered the flour from the mill He came in Jean-Pierre's bright blue lorry, but he drove slowly, and never hooted the hooter when he arrived, and he dumped the sacks of flour down on the pavement beside the trap-door without a smile.

One day, Marie-Céleste had to go to the mill-house to collect some things she had left there when they were decorating it. Paul-Paul went with her, although they had to walk, and it was a long way to go. When they arrived, they felt sadder than ever. The beautiful old house by the river looked so empty and forlorn. The garden was full of weeds, and inside the house, the new paint and wallpaper were covered with dust and cobwebs. There was no more groan . . . creak . . . splash! Groan . . . creak . . . splash! from the mill-wheel across the river. It had stopped turning, and no one but Jean-Pierre knew how to start it again. The moss and weed had grown thick on its paddles, and the rust was eating away at the great iron spokes and axles. Soon, if nothing was done, it would fall to pieces.

They saw Monsieur Dupré while they were there. He was still running the mill, but his hair had turned white, and he moved slowly about his work like an old man. 'My only son!' he kept saying. 'My only son!'

Marie-Céleste and Paul-Paul went back to Fleury-des-Bois feeling worse than ever.

But everyone else in Fleury-des-Bois felt quite differently about what had happened. Instead of being sad, they were angry. The day after Jean-Pierre should have married Marie-Céleste, there had been another photograph of him in the newspapers, holding up a silver trophy to show that he had won the big race in Italy. And there, at his side, had been Alphonse, grinning more than ever with triumph. This had made everyone furious. 'Just let that Jean-Pierre Dupré try to come back here now, if he dares!' they all said. 'We'll soon send him packing! Him and his grinning friend Alphonse!'

Nearly every week after that there was another photograph of Jean-Pierre in the newspapers. In each, the silver trophy he was holding up seemed bigger than the last, and in each, there was Alphonse at his shoulder, grinning and grinning. Each photograph made the people of Fleury-des-Bois angrier than ever.

'You forget all about that no-good Jean-Pierre!' they said to Marie-Céleste, when they went to buy bread and cakes at the Boulangerie. 'Mademoiselle Augustine was right about him all along. It's good riddance to bad rubbish!'

Even Oncle César and Tante Madeleine said the same. 'Don't waste your time pining for him!' they told Marie-Céleste. 'He'll never come back now, and it's time you forgot him.'

But Marie-Céleste didn't forget Jean-Pierre, and neither did Paul-Paul.

By now, the summer was ending. The cornfields out in the country were ripe and golden, rippling all the way to the horizon. Paul-Paul sometimes walked down to the level crossing by himself to look at them. One day he saw that the farmers were out with their harvesting machines, cutting the corn in long wide rows. Soon it would all be taken to the mill to be turned into flour. Jean-Pierre had called it treasure, and yet now he wasn't there to gather it in.

When Paul-Paul walked back from the level crossing, he could see the forest beyond the village, a beautiful russet-gold with autumn leaves. All the houses in Fleury-des-Bois were covered with red creeper again now, and the branches of the fruit-trees in the walled gardens were heavy laden with red apples and golden pears and pink peaches and purple plums. Paul-Paul picked up some of the fruit which had fallen into the back lanes and ate it. But nothing seemed the same, now that Jean-Pierre had gone.

Meanwhile, everyone else in Fleury-des-Bois was looking very cheerful. Romance was in the air once more, or so they hoped. There had been an incident at the café one evening recently which had caused quite a stir. One of the young men of the village had announced there, after a few glasses of wine, that he had always been secretly in love with Marie-Céleste, and now that Jean-Pierre was out of the way, he was going to try his luck with her. At this, several other young men had leapt to their feet and protested. No, each of them had declared, it was *he* who had been in love with her the longest, and it was therefore *he* who had the right to try first! There had nearly been a fight, until someone had sensibly shouted, 'Let's all try at once! And let the best man win!' And now they were all smartening themselves up and calling in at the Boulangerie one after another, to chat to Marie-Céleste, and ask her out for a walk or a drink at the café. Even Louis-Philippe, who was home on leave again at this time, started polishing his boots and buttons and brushing his Army uniform more than ever. And then, after a last, anxious look at his moustache in the hall mirror, to see if it had grown at all, off he would go to ask Marie-Céleste out too.

Everyone in Fleury-des-Bois started smiling again, as they wondered which of the young men Marie-Céleste would choose. They did all like a good wedding!

But Marie-Céleste didn't choose any of the young men. She

smiled and was friendly, and she even went out for walks and drinks at the café with them; but sooner or later she let all of them know that she was still in love with Jean-Pierre.

The young men kept trying for a while. Paul-Paul watched Louis-Philippe getting ready to go and see Marie-Céleste one evening. When he had finished, he looked himself up and down in the hall mirror, squaring his shoulders, and altering the tilt of his Army cap a little, and smoothing down his moustache. 'I'm not a bad-looking chap, really, am I?' he said to Paul-Paul, looking rather doubtfully at his own reflection. He leaned closer to the mirror, and then added, 'My moustache has definitely grown a bit, anyway. There's a girl in the Post Office who's taken quite a fancy to me. She blushes every time I go in there.' At this thought, Louis-Philippe gazed at his reflection with hope and pride. And then suddenly he took off his cap and threw it on the hall floor. 'Oh, what's the use!' he exclaimed. 'I'm no Jean-Pierre Dupré, with or without a moustache, and nor are any of the other chaps. Marie-Céleste's never going to get over him, so what's the use?' And then he picked up his cap, and put it back on his head, and said, 'I think I'll go and ask the girl at the Post Office out instead.'

Soon, one by one, all the other young men gave up too, and started going out with other girls.

This made Tante Madeleine very cross with Marie-Céleste. 'Jean-Pierre will never come back, you silly creature!' she cried. 'And meanwhile all the young men in the village will marry other girls, and you'll get left with no husband at all. You'll be an old maid, like Mademoiselle Augustine and Mademoiselle Ernestine!'

'I don't care!' cried Marie-Céleste. 'I *can't* forget Jean-Pierre, and that's that!'

After this, life was harder than ever for Marie-Céleste. Everyone in the village said she was being silly, and stopped feeling sorry for her. And her parents were cross with her, and no more young men came to the Boulangerie to ask her out. Only Paul-Paul stood by her. He still went to the Boulangerie whenever he could, and tried very hard to cheer her up. But often, when he arrived, he could see that she had been crying.

'Oh, Paul-Paul, you are a good friend, to come and see me so often!' she said to him one day. 'But you needn't, you know. Jean-Pierre never will come back, so I am just being silly.'

Paul-Paul didn't think that Jean-Pierre would ever come back either. After all, no one in Fleury-des-Bois thought so. But he said cheerfully, 'Never say never!' He remembered that she had said this to him once, when he had despaired of ever meeting a unicorn. It was true that he never had met a unicorn, but he had met Jean-Pierre instead, which had really been just as good. Perhaps something like that would happen to Marie-Céleste? 'Miracles do happen,' he added, remembering that she had said this to him too.

He hadn't expected this to make Marie-Céleste feel any better, but to his surprise she looked thoughtful, and after a moment she even smiled. 'You're right, Paul-Paul,' she said. 'Miracles do happen. I'd quite forgotten that.' And then she looked sad again, and said, 'But how could he come back now, even if he wanted to? He must know how angry everyone is with him. He probably thinks I'm angry too.'

Paul-Paul still didn't think Jean-Pierre would come back, but the answer to what Marie-Céleste had just said was easy.

'If he's brave enough to be a racing driver,' said Paul-Paul, 'he'd be brave enough to come back here!'

At this, Marie-Céleste laughed. 'Oh Paul-Paul, that's so true!' she said. 'I *am* silly not to have thought of that myself! And of course if he did come back, everyone would forgive him at once. People are like that. They'd probably soon feel proud of him.' And she added, 'I've been too unhappy to think straight, that's my trouble.' And then she looked sad again, and said, 'But will he ever *want* to come back, that's the real problem.'

To this Paul-Paul could think of no easy answer, and he looked sadly down into the bowl of cake-mix he was stirring. He realized that he had never thought properly about what had happened either – it had all been too terrible to think about. And there was so much that he couldn't understand, even now that he was really trying to. Had Jean-Pierre really loved Marie-Céleste or not? And if he had, why had he gone away? And if he hadn't, why had he asked her to marry him? And why had he got the mill-wheel working again, and called the corn treasure, if he didn't really care about the mill, and only cared about motor-racing? Was he a good person or a bad person? The more Paul-Paul thought about it all, the more muddled he felt.

'Never mind, Paul-Paul,' said Marie-Céleste, sounding much more like her old self than she had for weeks and weeks. 'I'll have a good think about it. You never know – there may be a solution to all this!'

After this, Marie-Céleste often looked very thoughtful instead of just unhappy. Sometimes she even looked quite hopeful, and said to herself, 'I wonder . . .?' And then she looked doubtful again, and said, 'Um, perhaps not.' She didn't tell Paul-Paul what she was thinking, but Paul-Paul couldn't help beginning to hope that Jean-Pierre would come back after all. He thought perhaps Jean-Pierre might come back for Christmas.

But Christmas came and went, and Jean-Pierre didn't come back.

One evening in January, Paul-Paul went to see Marie-Céleste quite late, just before supper-time.

All the shops were shut by this time, and the square was dark. There were no people or pigeons to be seen. It had been snowing, and the war memorial and the plane-trees and the benches all looked sepulchrally cold and white in the darkness. But Paul-Paul could see a light shining under the drawn blinds of the Boulangerie, and when he knocked on the door, Marie-Céleste opened it at once. She was just finishing work in her pastry-kitchen.

'Oh, Paul-Paul, I'm so glad you've come!' she said. 'I think I've got everything clear in my mind, at last, about Jean-Pierre. I understand now why he went away, and I think there *is* a chance that he'll come back one day, and marry me after all. Look, come with me. I've got something to show you which will help you understand too.'

She led Paul-Paul up two flights of stairs to her bedroom. Paul-Paul had never been there before. It was very pretty. It had a blue carpet, and a pattern of little blue rosebuds all over the wallpaper. There was a lovely old four-poster bed, with a canopy of white lace falling like a veil round the soft, white, lace-edged pillows. There was also a little dressing-table with an oval mirror, and a silver hairbrush and comb on it. And there was a wardrobe with all Marie-Céleste's dresses hanging up in it. Paul-Paul stroked the dresses, and then he stroked the silky blue curtains in the window. Outside, the snow was still falling in the darkness. It made Marie-Céleste's room seem very cosy.

Meanwhile Marie-Céleste had taken something out from under her pillows. It was a package tied up with a blue silk ribbon. She untied the ribbon, and took out from the package a lot of newspaper cuttings, which she laid out in a long row on her counterpane. They were all the photographs of Jean-Pierre which had been taken since he went away.

Marie-Céleste and Paul-Paul looked at the photographs in silence for a moment. Then Marie-Céleste said, 'If you wanted two different things, and you couldn't have them both, what would you do?'

'I'd choose between them, of course!' said Paul-Paul.

'But that might be difficult, mightn't it, if you wanted them both very badly?' said Marie-Céleste. 'You might need to think about it for a long time.'

'Yes,' agreed Paul-Paul.

'Well, Jean-Pierre wanted two different things very badly,' said Marie-Céleste. 'He wanted to marry me, but he also wanted to be a racing-driver. He couldn't have both, so he ought to have thought about it carefully, and then made his choice. But he didn't. Jean-Pierre's not a great thinker, you know. He likes to just rush into things, and hope for the best. And everything did happen so fast. When he first came here, I don't think he'd really made up his mind to settle down at the mill at all. Do you remember how sad he looked when my father asked him if he was settling down?'

'Yes,' said Paul-Paul 'But he fell in love with you at first sight, didn't he?'

'Yes,' said Marie-Céleste. 'And he asked me to marry him almost straight away, you know. I was the one who wanted time to think about it, not him. He wanted to rush into marriage, and worry about the motor-racing later. But that wasn't choosing properly, and it didn't work. When you choose properly between two things, you make up your mind to forget all about the thing you haven't chosen. But Jean-Pierre went on wishing he could be a racing-driver, so that the first time he was tempted, he gave in.'

'And has he chosen properly to be a racing-driver now?' asked Paul-Paul anxiously.

'Well, you look at the photographs and tell me,' said Marie-Céleste, with a smile.

Paul-Paul looked carefully at all the photographs, and then he noticed something about them which he had never noticed before. In all the photographs, Alphonse was grinning and grinning. But Jean-Pierre was hardly smiling at all in most of them, even though he had just won another race. And even in the photographs in which he was smiling, his eyes looked sad.

'No, he hasn't chosen properly to be a racing-driver!' shouted Paul-Paul excitedly. 'He's still thinking about you!'

'That's right,' said Marie-Céleste, with a happy smile.

'Then it's easy!' cried Paul-Paul eagerly. 'All we have to do is go and find him, and when he sees you he'll be very tempted, and – '

'No, Paul-Paul!' said Marie-Céleste, laughing. 'I thought of that too, but it won't do. He still wouldn't really have chosen properly, and then Alphonse would tempt him with another motorbike, and the same thing would happen again. He's got to think it out, and choose properly.'

'But couldn't we just go and talk to him, and persuade him?' asked Paul-Paul.

Marie-Céleste sighed. 'I'm afraid not, Paul-Paul,' she said. 'He's got to choose all by himself, of his own free will. Then he'll know he really means it, and so will we.'

'But *when* will he choose?' asked Paul-Paul, looking anxiously at the photographs, to see if there was any sign in Jean-Pierre's face that he was choosing.

'It might be a long time, Paul-Paul,' said Marie-Céleste. 'Or it might never happen. It's only fair to tell you that. Some people never do choose.'

'But isn't there anything we can *do*?' cried Paul-Paul.

Marie-Céleste gave another sigh. 'Only wait, and hope, I'm afraid,' she said. 'I'm sorry, Paul-Paul – I know that's difficult. But at least now you understand why Jean-Pierre went away, and what it is we have to wait and hope for.'

She began to gather up the photographs again, and put them carefully back into the package. Paul-Paul stood in the middle of the pretty blue room, lost in thought. Surely there must be some way of making Jean-Pierre choose? He understood that it would be no good persuading him, and that Jean-Pierre must think it out in his own mind, and make the choice himself. But if only there was some way of getting inside Jean-Pierre's mind, and putting the choice there! Paul-Paul shut his eyes tight, and tried to think if there was any way that he could do this.

'Tuwit-tuwoo, Paul-Paul!' called Marie-Céleste from the bedroom doorway. 'Come on! It's time you went home for your supper, and I've already called you three times!'

All through the time that Jean-Pierre had been away, Marie-Céleste and Paul-Paul had been going for walks in the forest on Saturday afternoons. Paul-Paul had seen the forest all white with snow, and the pool covered with ice. Then the snow and ice melted, and the sun began to get warmer again. And then one day they saw the first passion-flowers in the forest once more, and the week after that the whole floor of the forest was covered with them. All the fruit-trees in the gardens in Fleury-des-Bois were coming out into pink and white blossom, and it was nearly Easter. But still Jean-Pierre hadn't come back, and still Paul-Paul hadn't thought of a way of making him choose.

That afternoon, Paul-Paul gazed for a long time into the pool in the wildest depths of the forest. The reflections of the rocks and the silver birches and the bracken in the dark green water still looked just like a tapestry. Paul-Paul remembered how, a year ago, he had thought that if he only gazed deeply enough and long enough into the pool, he would somehow get back into the olden days, and meet a unicorn. Now, he couldn't help thinking that if he only gazed and gazed into the pool, somehow he would be able to get inside Jean-Pierre's mind and make him choose.

'Tuwit-tuwoo, Paul-Paul!' said Marie-Céleste. 'Time to go home! It's sunset.'

It was quite dark by the time Marie-Céleste and Paul-Paul reached the road. All the stars were out, beautifully glittering in the dark blue sky above Fleury-des-Bois. As they walked down the road, Paul-Paul was carrying the bunch of passion-flowers he had picked, to put by his unicorn picture when he got home, and he was looking at the stars. And then all of a sudden he saw a shooting star. It was big and white, with a long tail, and it fell and fell through the dark sky above Fleury-des-Bois.

'Look!' cried Paul-Paul. But Marie-Céleste was too late. She had been looking at the road, and by the time she looked up, the star had vanished.

'Never mind!' she said. 'So long as you remembered to wish.'

Paul-Paul had remembered to.

'What did you wish?' asked Marie-Céleste.

'You're not supposed to tell,' said Paul-Paul.

'I don't think it would matter if you told *me*,' said Marie-Céleste.

'I wished for Jean-Pierre to come back, of course!' said Paul-Paul.

'Oh, Paul-Paul, you are kind!' said Marie-Céleste. 'But you ought to wish for something for yourself.'

'But that *is* what I want most,' said Paul-Paul.

'All the same, you must have another wish,' said Marie-Céleste. 'Wish for something you really want badly, for yourself.'

'All right then,' said Paul-Paul. 'I wish I could go back into the olden days, and meet a unicorn.' He didn't really think now that this could ever happen, but then it wasn't a proper wish anyway. You couldn't have two wishes.

'Oh, Paul-Paul, do stop being so tiresome!' said Marie-Céleste, laughing. 'Don't you realize, I want you to wish for something I could give you! You've been such a good friend to me – a real friend! I want to give you a special present or a special treat in return.'

Paul-Paul thought for a bit. There was something he did want, something that Marie-Céleste had promised him once, a long time ago. But he thought that it might be too much to ask for just now, when Marie-Céleste was going through such a difficult time. 'Well,' he began doubtfully, 'you did say once that you'd take me to Paris to see the tapestries in the museum – '

'What a marvellous idea!' said Marie-Céleste, before he had finished speaking. 'Of course! Do you know, I'd quite forgotten I'd promised you that. But what a lovely idea! I'd like to see the tapestries again myself, and besides, it will do us both good to have an outing. Shall we go next Saturday?'

So they arranged to go the next Saturday. Paul-Paul was so excited, he could think of nothing else all that week.

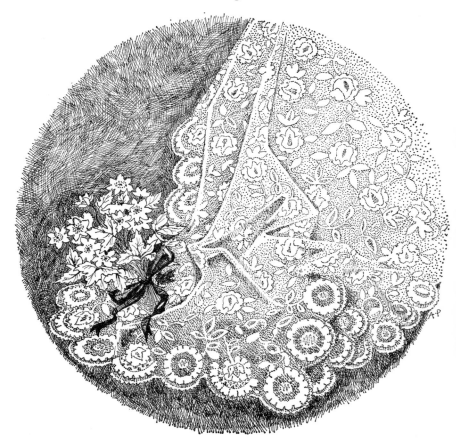

CHAPTER II

The tapestry museum

❦

At last next Saturday came, and Marie-Céleste and Paul-Paul set off for Paris early in the morning. Paul-Paul's mother and grandmother came to see them off at the station. Marie-Céleste was looking very pretty in her best blue dress, and her blue coat, and a straw hat with a blue ribbon round it, and Paul-Paul was wearing his new brown suit with long trousers.

Paul-Paul was very excited when the whistle blew and the train pulled out of the station. He had been for rides in trains once or twice before by this time, to visit his aunts and uncles in nearby towns and villages. But those had only been short journeys in little trains which kept stopping at every station. He had never been in a big express train like this before. How fast it went! It whizzed along with the great green forest flashing past on one side, and the great flat plain of open farmland flashing past on the other. Paul-Paul ran backwards and forwards between the corridor window and the compartment window on the other side of the train, where Marie-Céleste was sitting. He didn't want to miss anything. Once, when he was standing in the corridor, only a few minutes after they had left the station, the train went racing round a big bend in the railway line, and Paul-Paul saw Fleury-des-Bois in the distance behind them, nestling at the edge of the forest, with its church tower rising above the tree-tops. Already it looked very small. And then, as the train raced on round the big bend, it was whisked out of sight behind the trees.

Soon after this, they left the forest itself behind them, and the train rushed across the open plain, with fields and farms on either side of the railway line. Now and then the train gave a great long shriek of its whistle, and roared over a level crossing and through a village station, without even slowing down. Paul-Paul saw cars and lorries and cyclists waiting at the level crossings, and people standing on the station platforms, all flashing by so fast that they were only a blur. The villages all looked very like Fleury-des-Bois, with cobble-stoned streets leading down to the station, and grey stone houses with brown tiled roofs and walled gardens full of fruit-trees, clustered round a church with a tall grey tower.

But gradually, Paul-Paul noticed, after they had been travelling for quite a long time, the villages they passed through began to grow bigger, with lots of modern houses at their edges. The villages were also closer together than they had been before. Soon there began to be rows of houses by the railway line between the villages, instead of farmland. The gardens of the houses came right down to the railway line, and Paul-Paul could see house-wives hanging up their washing, and children playing in their sandpits. Paul-Paul thought it must be very strange to live with a railway line at the end of your garden, and dreadfully noisy too, especially at night, with express trains shrieking past all the time. But he supposed that the people who lived there had got used to it, just as he had got used to the owls hooting and the foxes yapping and howling in the forest.

All this time, Paul-Paul had been standing in the corridor. There was so much to look at. And now there began to be big factories by the railway line, and more and more houses. Soon there was no more country at all. It was like one endless village, going on and on and on.

Then Marie-Céleste called out from the compartment, 'Paul-Paul, come and look out on this side!'

Paul-Paul ran across to the compartment window. The train was just then swinging round another big curve in the railway line, so that he could see what was ahead. And there, stretching all the way to the horizon, and in every other direction as far as Paul-Paul could see, there were houses – miles and miles of grey and white houses with grey slate roofs, and amongst them, here and there, a church spire, or a big dome, or a cluster of green tree-tops, or the silver flash of a river. And in the middle, rising far above all the houses, was the Eiffel Tower. It was Paris!

Soon after this, the train pulled in to a very big station, and stopped. They were there!

Marie-Céleste and Paul-Paul had decided to spend the morning looking at Paris, and then go and see the tapestries after lunch. So off they went to look at the Eiffel Tower, and at lots of other big, famous buildings which Paul-Paul had learnt about at school. Paul-Paul was astonished to see what crowds and crowds of people there were everywhere in Paris, hurrying along the streets, and looking in the shop windows, and sitting in the pavement cafés. He was also amazed at how much traffic there was. There were hundreds and hundreds of cars and buses and lorries, driving three or four abreast, nose to tail, along all the streets, and all going just as fast as Jean-Pierre! There were also lots and lots of policemen at all the crossroads, waving their arms and blowing their shrill whistles all the time. It all made Paul-Paul feel quite overwhelmed.

But after Marie-Céleste and Paul-Paul had looked at all the famous buildings Paul-Paul had wanted to see, they went and sat in an old, quiet part of Paris, by the River Seine. Here, there were only cobble-stoned quays with weeping willows leaning out over the water, and a few old men with berets on their heads, fishing, and a few artists selling their pictures, and students browsing among the bookstalls by the quays. The traffic was no more than a distant rumble. Across the water from where Marie-Céleste and Paul-Paul were sitting, there was a beautiful big cathedral on an island, called Notre-Dame. With its white towers and turrets, and its white arches, and the water lapping all round it, overhung by weeping willows and trailing ivy, it looked just like a fairy-tale castle.

Marie-Céleste and Paul-Paul had lunch at a café on the island, next to the cathedral, and then they went to the tapestry museum. It was only a little way to walk from the cathedral, across a bridge over the River Seine, and up a wide, cobble-stoned boulevard with plane-trees along its pavements. Paul-Paul skipped happily along beside Marie-Céleste. He was going to see the tapestries with the unicorns in them at last!

*   *   *

The museum had once been a monastery, and it was one of the oldest buildings in Paris, Marie-Céleste told Paul-Paul. It had been built in the real olden days, more than a thousand years ago. They went in through a little pointed wood and iron door in an old, soot-blackened wall. The wall was covered with ivy, and the door creaked as they opened it. Just going through the door, thought Paul-Paul, was like going back into the olden days, and it was quite creepy.

Inside, they found themselves in a courtyard, with a big chestnut tree and a well in the middle. All round the courtyard there were high stone walls covered with ivy, with pointed stained-glass windows in them, and strange stone goblins perched on the window-sills and gutters. They had ugly grinning faces, and wings, and claws, and long snaky tails. They were called gargoyles, Marie-Céleste told Paul-Paul. Paul-Paul thought it was all very creepy indeed.

On the far side of the courtyard there was another door, with a ticket office into the museum itself. Marie-Céleste bought their tickets, and in they went.

There were hundreds of tapestries! Paul-Paul ran from room to room, looking at all of them. He saw battles, with knights on horseback fighting with bows and arrows and long lances, and he saw towns being besieged, with the townspeople pouring boiling oil down from the tops of the walls on to the enemy besieging them, and the enemy charging at the gates with battering rams. He saw ships in storms at sea, and brightly-coloured tents with dark-skinned men in them, wearing turbans and carrying strange, curved swords. He saw kings and queens, and pretty ladies combing their hair, and minstrels playing their musical instruments, and huntsmen hunting deer, and craftsmen weaving, and sawing wood, and making pots. He also saw lions and tigers, and elephants and camels, and monkeys. The only thing he didn't see anywhere, although he ran very fast from room to room, was a unicorn.

Paul-Paul ran back to Marie-Céleste, who was still looking at the tapestries in the first room by the ticket office.

'Marie-Céleste!' he cried. 'There *aren't* any unicorns!'

'Oh, Paul-Paul! Of course there are!' said Marie-Céleste. 'There are lots more tapestries upstairs, you know! Just let me finish looking at these, and then we'll go up there.'

Paul-Paul waited as patiently as he could, but Marie-Céleste seemed to want to look at every single stitch in every single tapestry she came to. She kept saying, 'Yes, yes, now we'll go upstairs, Paul-Paul!' And then, after walking only a few steps towards the stairs, she would stop in front of another tapestry, and say, 'Oh, do let's just look at this one first!'

But Paul-Paul had already looked at all of them, and he wanted to see a unicorn.

'Shall I go on ahead of you?' he asked.

'Yes, all right,' said Marie-Céleste. 'I shan't be long. And we'll easily find each other, because there are so few people here today.'

'See you in a minute!' said Paul-Paul, and off he ran up the stairs.

He ran up to the next floor, and through all the rooms there, but he didn't see any unicorns. So he ran up to the floor above that, but there were still no unicorns. So he ran up to the next floor, which was the top floor of the museum. There *had* to be some unicorns there!

But Paul-Paul ran through all the rooms on the top floor, and there were no unicorns.

Paul-Paul stopped in the middle of the very last room, and he nearly cried. He had come all the way to Paris, and there were no unicorns!

Then Paul-Paul saw an attendant in a dark blue uniform, sitting on a chair beside a door marked 'ENTRÉE INTERDITE', which means 'No Entry' in French. The attendant was an old man, and he seemed to be asleep. But while Paul-Paul was standing there looking at him, he opened one eye, and then shut it again.

'Excuse me, Monsieur,' said Paul-Paul politely, 'but aren't there any unicorns?'

'Whassat?' said the attendant, opening one eye again. He looked rather cross at being woken up.

'Aren't there any tapestries with unicorns in them, please, Monsieur?' said Paul-Paul.

'Only what you see,' said the attendant, in a bad-tempered voice, and he shut his eyes again.

Paul-Paul looked all the way round the room again, very slowly and carefully. But there were definitely no unicorns in any of the tapestries.

And then, while Paul-Paul was looking slowly round the room, he noticed that the door marked 'ENTRÉE INTERDITE' was slightly ajar. Perhaps there were some more tapestries in there, with unicorns in them?

Paul-Paul went back to the attendant again, and said, more politely than ever, 'Excuse me, please, Monsieur, but what's in there?'

The attendant slowly opened one eye again, and glared at Paul-Paul. Then, just as slowly, he lifted his hand, and pointed angrily at the notice on the door several times. 'ENTRÉE,' he said, 'INTERDITE! Can't you read? Are you a half-wit? ENTRÉE INTERDITE! And questions, also, INTERDITES! Now leave me in peace!'

Paul-Paul walked away to the other side of the room, and his heart was beating fast with anger. What a rude man! 'And I bet there are unicorns in there,' he thought. 'He's just too mean to tell me so.'

Paul-Paul stood at the far side of the room, and looked at the mysterious door. It was open just wide enough for him to see that inside there was a lovely dim, green, secret twilight, just like the dim green twilight in the forest at home. The more he looked at it, the more sure he felt that there was a unicorn in there. The only unicorn in the whole museum, and he wasn't allowed to see it!

By this time, the attendant had shut his eyes again, and seemed to be asleep. Paul-Paul began to have a very brave idea. He was going to creep past the attendant, and go into that secret room!

Paul-Paul stood very still, hardly daring to breathe, waiting to make sure that the attendant was really asleep. It was very quiet. There seemed to be no one else at all on the top floor except the attendant and Paul-Paul. 'Marie-Céleste must still be looking at the tapestries on one of the lower floors,' thought Paul-Paul, and now he was glad that she was taking so long to look at everything.

The attendant's eyes were still closed, and he was breathing slowly and deeply. And then, as Paul-Paul watched, his head fell back against the wall behind him, and he let out a loud snore.

Paul-Paul tiptoed very, very quietly across the room. He reached the secret door without making a sound, and stood right beside the sleeping attendant, with his hand on the door-handle. His heart was beating faster and faster. He prayed that the door wouldn't creak; and then, very, very gently, he opened it wider. It made no sound. Paul-Paul opened it just wide enough for him to slip inside, and then he carefully closed it again behind him.

He was inside the secret room!

CHAPTER 12

In the secret room

♣

PAUL-PAUL looked round him. At first, the green twilight in the room was so dim, he couldn't see anything at all. But soon his eyes grew used to it, and he saw that he was in a round room, with a pointed roof and no windows. The only light came from a small round skylight in the centre of the roof. Its glass was thick and green, which partly explained the greenness of the twilight.

But there was also another reason for this greenness. As Paul-Paul's eyes grew more and more used to the twilight, he saw that there was a long tapestry going all round the walls of the round room, whose background was dark green. There were some paler shapes in it too, but at first Paul-Paul couldn't make out what they were, so he tiptoed closer. Then he saw that they were silver birches; and there were some brown shapes too, which were the trunks of other trees. And then he tiptoed closer still, and saw that the dark green background of the tapestry was covered all over with little white passion-flowers!

Paul-Paul tiptoed even closer, and saw that the tapestry was very threadbare in places, and very faded too. He realized that it must be very, very old.

'But if it's very old,' thought Paul-Paul, 'there *must* be a unicorn in it somewhere!' And he leaned closer still in the hope of seeing one. Ah! What was that white shape among the branches above his head? Paul-Paul stood on tiptoe, and saw that it was a little white owl, sitting on a branch, and seeming to look at him in a friendly way. But what was that other white shape, glimmering from far away through the trees? A unicorn? Or a castle? Paul-Paul thought it was probably a castle, but the tapestry was so faded, and the light so dim, and the white shape so far away through the trees, that he couldn't be sure.

So he leaned closer, and closer, and closer . . .

It *was* a castle!

The green twilight seemed to have grown a little brighter all of a sudden, as if the sun had come out from behind a cloud. Yes! There were rays of golden sunlight slanting down now through the trees, and the sun was shining brightly on the castle in the distance. Paul-Paul could see all its glistening white turrets, and its little pointed windows, and the silver circle of the moat all round it. A real castle! Paul-Paul began to run through the trees towards it.

But after only a few steps, he stopped suddenly. 'I mustn't run in a tapestry!' he thought. 'I might tear it! I might be lucky and not get punished for coming into this room, but if I tear the tapestry I certainly will be! I'd better go back at once!'

And after a last, wistful look at the castle, Paul-Paul turned round to go back the way he had come.

But where was the secret room? Whichever way Paul-Paul looked, all he could see was miles and miles of forest trees stretching away into the distance, with the ground beneath them spangled with passion-flowers. Oh, how pretty it was! It was just like the forest at home, except that everything was made with hundreds and hundreds of tiny stitches. As Paul-Paul looked all round him, he quite forgot for the moment that he was supposed to be finding his way back to the secret room. There was so much to look at here!

As Paul-Paul looked closer at everything around him, he began to notice all sorts of lovely little details which he hadn't seen at first. The trunks and branches of the trees, for instance, weren't just plain strips of brown or silver, as they would have been if Paul-Paul had painted them. Every little seam and knot in the bark had been sewn in different shades of brown or silver, so that the trees looked exactly like real trees. And when Paul-Paul looked up, he saw that every separate twig and leaf had been carefully sewn with different shades of green and brown. He could even see the veins in the leaves. And among the leaves, there were little yellow catkins here and there, and silver pussy-willow purses. And on the ground, when he looked down, he saw that the dark green floor of the forest had been sewn with every leaf and blade of grass stitched separately. Even the tiny purple veins in the white petals of the passion-flowers were there. Nothing had been left out! Paul-Paul heaved a deep sigh as he looked at it all. *Now* he understood why Marie-Céleste had wanted to stop and look at every single stitch in every tapestry!

Paul-Paul knew that he shouldn't really touch anything, but he couldn't resist stroking the tree beside him, just once. And then he thought, 'That's funny!' For although he could feel all the tiny stitches under his fingers, at the same time the bark felt quite hard and rough. He reached up and gently touched a leaf on a branch above his head, and again he could feel the tiny stitches, but he could also feel the leaf's cool, velvety dampness. And when he bent down and touched one of the passion-flowers growing by his feet, sure enough, its petals felt all cool and silky.

'The person who made this tapestry was very clever!' thought Paul-Paul. 'Everything not only looks real, but it feels real too!'

Just then, Paul-Paul noticed a little brown rabbit hiding amongst the leaves at his feet. It was so cleverly hidden that it had taken him all this time to notice it. Paul-Paul longed to stroke it. 'But if I do,' he thought sadly, 'it'll only run away.' And then he remembered: 'It *can't* run away! It's only a tapestry rabbit!'

So Paul-Paul bent down and gently stroked the rabbit, and of course it didn't move. Yet its fur felt warm and soft, and he was almost sure that he could feel its body quivering under his fingers, just as if it were really alive.

'That's *funny*!' thought Paul-Paul.

There certainly was something very strange about this tapestry. For when Paul-Paul straightened up again, he suddenly noticed that there were lots and lots of little brown rabbits in the under-growth all round him, which he hadn't seen there last time he looked. There was also a beautiful russet-gold fox standing and looking at him, with one forepaw raised, from a clearing between the trees only a few yards away. Paul-Paul was sure it hadn't

been there last time he looked. And then he saw that there was a herd of deer beside the moat of the castle, bending their heads to drink. And he was sure that they hadn't been there either, a moment ago. The only creature he had seen when he first looked at the tapestry was the friendly little white owl. The owl was still there, perched on a branch just above Paul-Paul's head, and it was still looking at Paul-Paul with a very friendly expression. But all the other branches of the trees, which Paul-Paul was quite sure had been bare only a moment ago, were now covered with all sorts of other birds too, as well as lots of squirrels.

'Well, either I didn't look properly before,' thought Paul-Paul, 'or all these birds and animals have been creeping closer while I wasn't looking!'

The more Paul-Paul looked at them all, the more sure he was that they *had* been creeping closer while he wasn't looking. They were very still, it was true. But they were *too* still. They were as still as you are when you're playing Grandmother's Footsteps!

Paul-Paul looked all round him, and everything was very, very still. Not a leaf, nor a flower, nor a catkin stirred, and nor did any of the birds or animals.

'I must have made a mistake,' thought Paul-Paul sadly. 'Of course things can't move in a tapestry. And now I really must go back to the secret room, before I tear something.'

Paul-Paul turned away, and as he did so he noticed something funny about his feet. He was wearing his party shoes! His shiny black party shoes with silver buckles on them!

'I must have put them on by mistake this morning, instead of my best brown walking shoes, because I was so excited about coming to Paris!' thought Paul-Paul. 'And Maman and Grand'-mère never noticed! And I came all the way to Paris in them, and Marie-Céleste never noticed either! How silly of us all!'

But even while Paul-Paul was having a good laugh about it, he was thinking, 'But that's funny! I *did* put on my best brown walking shoes this morning. I distinctly remember that I did. Where can they have gone?'

Paul-Paul began looking anxiously for them in the under-growth. But even while he was looking, he noticed something even stranger about himself. He wasn't wearing his new brown suit with long trousers any more either. He was wearing the page-boy suit which Marie-Céleste had made him for her wedding – his blue velvet page-boy suit, with its white lace cuffs and white lace collar! He certainly hadn't been wearing *that* when he set out from Fleury-des-Bois that morning!

'Oh dear!' thought Paul-Paul, feeling very worried. 'Whatever will Maman say, if I've lost my new brown suit as well as my best walking shoes?'

But before Paul-Paul could even begin to look for his suit, he noticed something even more extraordinary. His page-boy suit and his party shoes were all sewn with tiny stitches, just as if they were part of a tapestry! Even the silver buckles on his shoes were made of tiny stitches. And then he noticed that his own skin was made of tiny stitches too! And so was his hair, when he reached his hand up to feel it! He could feel all the tiny stitches under his fingers, but at the same time his hair still felt like hair. And his skin still felt like skin, too, and the velvet and lace of his page-boy suit still felt like velvet and lace. Even his shoes still felt like patent leather, when he bent down to feel them, and the buckles still felt like metal. And he could still wiggle his toes inside his shoes.

'Well, thank goodness for that!' thought Paul-Paul. And then he added to himself, 'Still, all the same, there's no doubt about it, I've turned into a tapestry boy!'

For a moment, Paul-Paul wasn't quite sure if he was pleased about this. 'How am I going to turn back into a real boy again, and go home to Fleury-des-Bois?' he wondered.

But then he looked at the castle in the distance again, and he had a sudden happy thought. 'If I'm a tapestry boy now,' he realized, 'I can run about, and touch everything, and do just what I like, without tearing anything! One piece of tapestry can't tear another piece of tapestry! I could even climb a tree if I wanted to! And I can go to the castle after all! I'll think about how to turn back into a real boy later, but first I'll go to the castle. There might be a unicorn there! Oh, whoopee!' And he began to dance about with excitement.

But while he was dancing about, he suddenly had another happy thought – one which made him stop dancing at once, and stand very still, looking carefully all about him.

'If I'm a tapestry boy, and yet I can dance about,' he said to himself, 'then all these tapestry birds and animals must be able to move too. They *were* creeping closer while I wasn't looking!'

And Paul-Paul looked round at all the birds and animals, to see if he could see any of them moving. But they were all completely still.

'Oh, please come to life!' he whispered to them. 'I won't hurt you. I only want to make friends.'

Paul-Paul looked all round him. Everything in the tapestry forest remained very still. Then, very gently, a breeze came rustling through the trees. The sunlight grew brighter, and all the leaves began to dance. A catkin fell near his feet. Then, one after another, the animals stirred, and began to come towards him. The rabbits came hopping through the undergrowth to his feet, and the birds flew and settled on the branches round him. The squirrels leapt towards him from tree to tree, and the fox came trotting through the trees. Even the deer in the distance lifted their heads from drinking at the castle moat, and came towards him.

'Oh!' cried Paul-Paul in delight, as all the birds and animals crowded round him. How friendly they all were! The birds and squirrels perched on his shoulders, the fox and the deer pushed their noses into his hands, and the rabbits stood on their hind legs at his feet, begging to be picked up. Paul-Paul stroked and cuddled all of them, but still they all crowded round him, begging for more.

But the more Paul-Paul stroked all the birds and animals, the more it began to seem to him that they were trying to tell him something. Their dark eyes seemed unhappy and frightened, and they seemed to be begging him for help.

'Oh, what is it?' cried Paul-Paul, as the birds and animals gazed pleadingly at him. 'Do you want me to help you with something?'

At this, the fox yapped and the birds twittered; and the little white owl, which was still sitting on a branch above Paul-Paul's head, hooted, 'Tuwit-tuwoo!' To his delight, Paul-Paul found he could understand what they were saying. And although the rabbits and the squirrels and the deer only went on gazing dumbly at him, Paul-Paul understood what they were feeling too, and trying to tell him. They were all saying, 'Yes!'

'Oh, I'll do anything to help you!' cried Paul-Paul. 'Just tell me what it is, and I'll do it straight away!'

But all the birds and animals looked sadly at Paul-Paul. They all seemed to be saying, 'You won't be able to. It's too difficult and dangerous.'

'But tell me what it is!' cried Paul-Paul.

At this, the little white owl hooted, 'Tuwit-tuwoo!' Then he rose from his branch, circled three times round Paul-Paul's head, and began to fly slowly away between the trees towards the castle, looking back now and then over his shoulder at Paul-Paul. He wanted Paul-Paul to follow him to the castle!

So Paul-Paul set off through the trees towards the castle, and all the birds and animals went with him. The birds flew round his head, and the squirrels leapt from tree to tree above him, while the fox and the rabbits and deer ran along at his side. And all the way the little white owl flew just ahead of him, hooting, 'Tuwit-tuwoo! Tuwit-tuwoo!' as it flew.

Paul-Paul wondered very much what he was going to find at the castle.

CHAPTER 13

The castle

❧

As he approached the castle, Paul-Paul thought it seemed a very sad place. The weeping willows at the edge of the moat seemed to droop sadly over the water, and the chains of the drawbridge were rusty, and its wooden planks green with moss and weed. The beautiful white turrets of the castle were beginning to crumble into ruins, and ivy was beginning to creep all over them. Everything looked very forlorn and neglected, and there was no sign of life.

When they reached the drawbridge, all the animals and birds hung back. They seemed to be saying, 'We'll wait here for you.' Only the little white owl flew on over the drawbridge, hooting, 'Tuwit-tuwoo!' Paul-Paul followed him.

The little white owl led Paul-Paul through a big open doorway with a rusty portcullis, and into an inner courtyard. The paving-stones of the courtyard were cracked, and there was grass growing between them. Now that Paul-Paul was within the castle walls, the place seemed more silent and deserted than ever.

But the owl flew across the courtyard, and disappeared through a little pointed door on the far side. Paul-Paul followed.

Paul-Paul found himself following the owl up a narrow spiral staircase. Up and up they went, for a very long time. There was thick dust on all the stone steps, and cobwebs in all the corners. It looked as if no one had gone up or down those stairs for centuries. Where *was* the owl leading him, and why?

At last they reached the top, and Paul-Paul found himself standing before a little pointed wooden door. It was so grey with dust and veiled with cobwebs that it was almost invisible. Paul-Paul could see from the dust on the latch that the door hadn't been opened for years and years. There couldn't possibly be anyone in there. And yet the little white owl was hovering above the door, hooting 'Tuwit-tuwoo!' He wanted Paul-Paul to open the door and go in!

Paul-Paul lifted the dusty latch, and the door opened with a groan of its rusty hinges. His heart was beating fast. Whatever was he going to find in there?

Paul-Paul found himself in a little round turret room with a pointed roof. All round it, there were little pointed windows, curtained with cobwebs. Through the cobwebs, he could just glimpse a view of the forest, stretching away for miles and miles. Then he looked round the room.

Everything in the room was so covered with dust and cobwebs that at first he could hardly make out anything at all. But soon he saw a four-poster bed in one corner, grey with dust and canopied with lace and cobwebs. And then he saw a dressing-table in another corner, with an oval mirror which was so dusty that its glass was quite blank. Under the dust on the dressing-table he could just make out the shapes of a silver hairbrush and comb, which were almost buried. And in the middle of the little round room there was a dusty weaving loom, with the dusty statue of a princess sitting beside it, one hand resting on the loom, and her head drooping sadly.

Paul-Paul thought it was the saddest place he had ever seen. 'Why ever did the owl want to bring me here?' he wondered. If only the princess sitting by the loom had been real, and not just a statue!

But just as Paul-Paul thought this, a little breeze wafted in through the turret windows, fluttering the curtains of cobwebs and stirring the dust on all the surfaces. The statue by the loom gave a sigh and lifted her head. 'Ah, at last you've come!' she said. 'I've been waiting for you for a thousand years!'

It *was* a real princess! Paul-Paul fell to one knee at once before her.

Meanwhile the gentle little breeze was still blowing in through the windows, blowing the dust off the princess; and as she stirred and passed her hand over her face, more dust fell from her. Little by little, Paul-Paul saw her beautiful face grow clear, and then her long fair hair, crowned with a chaplet of passion-flowers, and her dress, which was made of white lace, with a long, long train. It looked like a wedding dress to Paul-Paul.

'At last! At last!' said the princess, when all the dust had fallen from her. 'Now we shall be saved!' Then she sighed, and added, 'I thought you were never going to come!'

'Are you sure you mean *me*?' asked Paul-Paul doubtfully. How could anyone have been waiting for *him* for a thousand years?

'Yes, you!' said the princess. 'Only you are brave enough to save us! Only you believe enough in unicorns!'

Paul-Paul wasn't at all sure if he *was* brave, although it was true that he had crept past that rude, angry attendant in the museum, and into the secret room. But at the mention of unicorns, he forgot all about whether he was brave or not.

'Yes, yes!' he said eagerly. 'What is it you want me to do?'

'Come closer, and I'll explain,' said the princess. And she beckoned him to come and look at the big loom beside her.

Paul-Paul stood looking at the loom, while the little white owl came and perched on the edge of it. Paul-Paul could see that the princess had been sewing a tapestry. But the tapestry was still so grey with dust that Paul-Paul couldn't make out anything in it.

'I was going to be married to a handsome prince,' the princess began to explain, blowing the dust gently off the tapestry as she spoke. Gradually Paul-Paul began to be able to make out a white castle with a moat round it, in the middle of a great green forest. 'The prince was brave and kind and gay, and he loved me,' the princess went on, 'but he had a passion for going hunting in the forest. He loved to get on his horse and go galloping away very fast, galloping and galloping all day! I was worried that he would have an accident, so I made him promise that he wouldn't go hunting any more. But he had a friend, the black baron, who was a very bad influence on him; and one day the black baron persuaded the prince to go hunting in the forest with him, just one last time. Look, here they are setting off together.'

All the time she had been speaking, the princess had been gently blowing the dust off the tapestry, and now Paul-Paul could see everything in it clearly. He could see two horsemen riding out over the drawbridge of the castle into the forest. One horse was white, and on it rode the handsome prince. He had fair hair, and merry blue eyes, and he was smiling and waving goodbye. But the other horse was black, and on it rode the black baron. He was dark and ugly, and he was grinning triumphantly to himself as the two of them rode away. The princess was waving goodbye to them from a turret window.

'I wasn't worried,' said the princess sadly. 'The prince had promised me that it was the very last time he'd ever go hunting, and he had promised that he wouldn't gallop fast. I sat here all day, singing happily to myself and sewing, waiting for them to come home. But they never did.'

She paused to wipe away a tear, then went on, 'I waited and waited, and I couldn't understand what had happened. And then this little owl, who flies through the forest day and night, came and told me everything. The black baron had turned the prince into a unicorn! All day and all night, now, he gallops round and round in the forest, as fast as he can.'

'And you want me to go and catch him!' cried Paul-Paul eagerly. 'Of course I'll do that for you! I'll go at once!' And he began to run from the room.

'Wait!' said the princess. 'There are dangers that I must warn you about. First of all, you must realize that unicorns are very fierce and wild. They don't want to be caught, and they often kill people who try to catch them, especially people who are carrying weapons. There is only one way to catch a unicorn. You must go to the wildest depths of the forest, unarmed. And then, if you really love unicorns very much, instead of killing you, the unicorn might become tame at the sight of you. But even that isn't certain.'

At this, Paul-Paul swallowed hard. But already the princess was adding, 'And there's another danger, which is much worse. The black baron has turned himself into a dreadful dragon. He lives in a cave in the wildest depths of the forest, rumbling and breathing fire all day and all night. He kills anyone who goes near the unicorn. He flies through the air with his great black wings, snatching with his sharp claws and snapping with his wicked jaws, and belching out foul smoke and fire. Nothing has ever been able to escape him!'

This settled the whole matter as far as Paul-Paul was concerned. He definitely wasn't going anywhere near the wildest depths of the forest, unicorn or no unicorn! He had other things to think about, like getting back to Marie-Céleste and Fleury-des-Bois!

But meanwhile the princess was warning him about yet another danger. 'If you *did* manage to find the unicorn without the dragon killing you first, and you *did* manage to tame him, then you would have to fight the dragon to the death. The dragon must die, or he will destroy the whole forest, and even this castle, to get his revenge. But he's so huge and so savage, I doubt if it's possible to kill him. Still, you would have to make the attempt.'

This settled the matter more than ever, as far as Paul-Paul was concerned. He was going home at once! All the same, as he began to turn away, he couldn't help asking, 'I suppose, if I *did* get as far as fighting the dragon, I'd be riding on the unicorn's back at the time?' He did love to hear about riding unicorns!

'Of course,' answered the princess. 'You would have a much better chance of killing the dragon then. The unicorn's horn could act as your sword – for remember that you would have no other weapon. In fact, some people say that the unicorn's horn is the *only* weapon that can kill the dragon.'

'I see,' said Paul-Paul, dreamily. 'And after I'd killed the dragon, I'd have a long gallop on the unicorn's back, I suppose – all the way back here to the castle?'

'That's right,' said the princess. 'And then, when you crossed the drawbridge, and the unicorn saw me again, at once he would turn back into the prince, and we would live happily ever after.'

Paul-Paul stood blinking and blinking as he imagined himself galloping through the forest on the unicorn's back. How wonderful it would have been! If only he was brave enough to go and catch the unicorn! If only there wasn't a dragon!

'Tuwit-tuwoo!' hooted the owl. Paul-Paul woke up from his day-dream with a start, and noticed that the owl and the princess were both looking at him with happy, grateful faces.

'Oh, how brave you are!' cried the princess admiringly. 'I've described great dangers to you, yet you've never even flinched! You've only asked more questions, brushing the danger aside! How *very* brave you must be!' And before Paul-Paul could say a word, she took both his hands in hers, and added, 'How can I ever thank you enough? If you had refused to go, we might have had to wait another thousand years for someone who really believed in unicorns to come and save us. We might have had to wait for

ever. And, as you can see, the forest is already beginning to fade away and die. If it weren't for you, I don't think we would ever have been saved.'

Paul-Paul looked at the princess and the owl, and went very pink. The princess hadn't understood! He had only wanted to hear about riding unicorns! But after this, he didn't see how he could possibly refuse to go – or at any rate not to the princess's face. 'I'll pretend I'm going to go,' he decided, 'and then, as soon as I'm out of the castle, I'll run away. I'll get back to the secret room again somehow, and then home to Fleury-des-Bois as fast as I can, and I'll never think about unicorns again!'

But meanwhile the princess had taken the chaplet of passion-flowers off her head, and was quickly unthreading it. She made the flowers into a bunch, which she tied together with a blue ribbon from her hair, and then gave it to Paul-Paul, saying, 'Here, take these! They will help you in your dangerous mission. They will give you courage and hope, and they will also help you to tame the unicorn. The dragon has cast a spell over his mind, so that he does nothing but gallop round and round in circles without thinking. But when he sniffs these flowers, the spell will be broken. He will be able to think again, and choose what he wants to do for the rest of his life. He may choose to go on galloping round and round, and in that case he will kill you, and trample these flowers underfoot. But if he chooses to come home and marry me, and be prince of this castle again, he will kneel down and put his head in your lap, and take the passion-flowers in his mouth. At that moment he will become transformed and perfectly tame, and do everything you wish. He will kill the dragon if he can – and these flowers will give him strength and daring – and then he will come galloping home. And when I see him coming, with these flowers in his mouth, I shall know that he has really chosen me for ever. And now go, and Godspeed! The owl will go with you, and always lead the way.'

'Tuwit-tuwoo!' hooted the owl. And he rose from the edge of the loom, and flew out through the pointed wooden door.

Paul-Paul followed the owl down the spiral staircase, carrying the bunch of passion-flowers in his hand, and shivering with fright. He knew now that he would *have* to go to the wildest depths of the forest, and try to catch the unicorn, and brave the dreadful dragon. He couldn't just throw the passion-flowers on the ground and run away. They were the princess's wedding chaplet, and a sacred trust. There was no escape!

CHAPTER 14

The dragon and the unicorn

♣

On the other side of the drawbridge, all the birds and animals were waiting for Paul-Paul. They made quite a large crowd. Paul-Paul realized that even if he had still been planning to run away, it would have been quite impossible, with so many onlookers. And when he had crossed the drawbridge, they all crowded eagerly round him, perching on his shoulders, and pushing their noses into his hand, and rubbing their heads against him, to show how grateful they were that he was going to try and rescue their prince. The fact that they were all counting on Paul-Paul made him feel a little bit braver.

Meanwhile, the little white owl had circled three times round the highest castle turret, and now he swooped down and hovered just above Paul-Paul's head. 'Tuwit-tuwoo!' he hooted, and then he began to fly away through the trees into the depths of the forest, looking back now and then to see if Paul-Paul was following.

Paul-Paul took a deep breath, clutched the bunch of passion-flowers tightly in his hand, and set off into the forest after the owl. All the birds and animals went with him.

'Ah, that's nice!' thought Paul-Paul. 'If they're all coming too, I shan't feel nearly so frightened.' And he felt almost cheerful as they all went deeper and deeper into the forest.

For quite a long way, the forest was just as pretty as it had been when Paul-Paul had first come into it. The sunlight slanted down through the trees, and the ground was covered with passion-flowers. It was quite hard to believe that there really was a dragon.

But gradually the white glimmer of the castle grew fainter and fainter through the trees in the distance behind them, and then at last it disappeared altogether. Meanwhile the undergrowth began to grow thicker and darker and more tangly, and there were strange, creepy rustlings in the bushes, and sudden harsh squawks and flappings, as great black birds rose from the branches of the trees, and glided away with eerie clanking noises. Soon, a lot of the animals and birds which had been keeping Paul-Paul company began to look very frightened, and lagged behind. And then, one by one, they hung their heads, and turned round and crept away, back towards the safety of the castle. 'We're very sorry,' they seemed to be saying, 'but we're not as brave as you are. We're too frightened to come any further.'

Before long, the only animal which hadn't run away was the fox. He seemed to be braver than the others. He still trotted along at Paul-Paul's side, with his head held proudly high, and his beautiful bushy tail waving behind him. 'I'm the bravest animal in the forest!' he told Paul-Paul, in his yapping language. '*I* won't run away and desert you, like all those cowardly birds and squirrels and rabbits and deer – not me!' And Paul-Paul walked on, following the little white owl, with his hand resting on the fox's warm, furry neck. He was very glad that he still had one friend keeping him company. It made all the difference.

Meanwhile, the path they were following grew narrower and narrower and darker and darker. There were no flowers covering the ground any more, but only thick undergrowth, and rocks, and rotten tree-trunks, and poisonous toadstools. And there were no more rays of sunlight slanting down through the trees, and no beautiful dim green twilight, but only a swirling dark grey fog – or was it smoke? – which seemed to be growing blacker every moment. And Paul-Paul noticed that the trees, which had been growing more faded and threadbare all the way, were now beginning to be scorched and blackened with charred, leafless branches, as if there had been a fire. They were approaching the dragon's cave!

Then, all of a sudden, a dreadful rumble came out of the gloom ahead! It grew louder and louder, and the ground shook under Paul-Paul's feet. A great cloud of black smoke swirled towards him through the trees.

The fox let out a yowl of terror, tucked his bushy tail between his legs, and turned and fled back the way they had come, howling as he went. Even the little white owl gave a shrill hoot of fright, and flew up high above the tree-tops to safety. Paul-Paul was alone!

Paul-Paul's legs were shaking so much he could hardly stand up. The thick black smoke was swirling all round him, so that he was choking from its horrible taste, and his eyes were smarting and watering. But he clutched the bunch of passion-flowers more tightly than ever in his hand, and stayed his ground.

And then, while he stood there, blinded and choking, he heard something crashing through the undergrowth towards him! He was too terrified to move. Closer and closer it came – he could see the trees and bushes swaying and bending in its path. And now he could see a great white shape in the clouds of black smoke, leaping through the bushes towards him. 'That's funny!' he just had time to think. 'It's white! I thought dragons were always black, or green.'

And then the clouds of smoke went swirling away, and Paul-Paul saw that it wasn't the dragon at all. It was the unicorn!

The rumbling had stopped now, and the ground was still under Paul-Paul's feet. Gradually the black smoke drifted away through the trees, and even a pale ray of sunlight came slanting down into the clearing where Paul-Paul and the unicorn stood facing each other.

The unicorn pawed the ground, and lowered his head threateningly at Paul-Paul. But Paul-Paul wasn't afraid. He didn't care what happened now, for he had really met a unicorn at last!

How beautiful the unicorn was! His white coat was gleaming, and his sharp white horn was shining in the sun, and his long white tail was waving splendidly behind him. Paul-Paul laughed for sheer joy at the sight of him. And then he remembered the passion-flowers, and held the bunch out for the unicorn to sniff.

At the sight of the passion-flowers, the unicorn's blue eyes, which had been clouded with fierceness, suddenly became bright and clear and sharp. 'The spell's breaking already!' thought Paul-

Paul excitedly. 'He's beginning to think again! But which will he choose? – to go back to the castle and marry the princess, or to go on being a unicorn, and kill me?'

But before Paul-Paul had time to feel either hopeful or frightened, the unicorn gave a loud, rebellious snort; and then, with a wild toss of his head, he leapt out of the clearing and galloped away through the trees and out of sight.

Paul-Paul ran a few steps after the unicorn, and then stopped in the middle of the clearing. 'It's no use chasing him,' he thought sadly. 'He gallops so fast, I could never catch him. And besides, he's chosen to go on being a unicorn, so what's the use?' Paul-Paul realized that he had been lucky that the unicorn hadn't killed him, but he felt too sad to care about that.

'He's gone already, and I'll never see him again!' he thought. And he stood in the middle of the clearing, filled with despair.

But while he stood there, he heard a thundering of hoofs in the distance again, coming closer and closer through the trees. Then suddenly the unicorn leapt over the bushes into the clearing again, and began to gallop wildly round and round Paul-Paul.

'He's come back to kill me after all!' thought Paul-Paul. And now he felt very frightened indeed.

Round and round him galloped the unicorn. After a while, Paul-Paul began to wonder why he hadn't been killed yet. And then he noticed that all the time the unicorn was galloping round him, he was looking at the bunch of passion-flowers out of the corner of his bright blue eye.

'Perhaps he's going to change his mind!' thought Paul-Paul excitedly. And he held out the passion-flowers towards the unicorn, turning round and round in circles where he stood.

Faster and faster galloped the unicorn, looking at the passion-flowers all the time. Sometimes his bright blue eye looked longingly at them, and he galloped very close, flaring his nostrils to sniff. And then his eye would turn hard and fierce, and he would gallop on again.

Gradually the unicorn galloped in smaller and smaller circles round Paul-Paul. Paul-Paul was growing quite giddy from turning round and round where he stood. The unicorn was so close now that when he tossed his head, his sharp horn only missed Paul-Paul by inches.

Then suddenly the unicorn stopped. With a great whinnying noise he reared up in front of Paul-Paul, his forelegs pawing the air. And then down he came, bending his head and pointing his sharp white horn straight at Paul-Paul's heart. He had chosen to go on being a unicorn, and he was going to kill Paul-Paul.

Paul-Paul fell to his knees before the unicorn, holding out the passion-flowers in one last hope.

Step by step the unicorn came closer, until the sharp tip of his horn was touching Paul-Paul's chest. Still Paul-Paul held out the passion-flowers, so that they were right under the unicorn's nose. The unicorn's nostrils flared as he sniffed them, and slowly his bright blue eyes changed. The wild fierceness faded from them, and they became thoughtful, and steady, and deep. And then, at last, he knelt down before Paul-Paul, and took the passion-flowers gently in his mouth.

'Oh, unicorn, unicorn!' cried Paul-Paul happily, stroking the unicorn's handsome white head and his strong white neck, and his ears, and his sharp white horn, and putting his arms round the unicorn's neck and hugging him. The unicorn rubbed his head gently against Paul-Paul, and pushed his nose into Paul-Paul's hand, and laid his head in his lap. And all the time he was holding the passion-flowers in his mouth, and his blue eyes were warm and loving.

'Oh, unicorn!' said Paul-Paul. 'You've really chosen to go home and become a prince again, and marry the princess, haven't you?'

The unicorn gave a little whinny and nodded his head.

'And you'll never run away again, will you?' said Paul-Paul.

And the unicorn gave another little whinny and shook his head.

Paul-Paul was so happy, he had quite forgotten about the dragon. But just then there was a low, ominous rumble from not very far away, and a whiff of black smoke came drifting through the trees. The little white owl came gliding quickly down from above the tree-tops, and perched on a branch at the edge of the

clearing. 'Tuwit-tuwoo!' he hooted. 'Quickly, climb on the unicorn's back! The dragon's coming! That rumbling and smoking
a little while ago was only the dragon snoring in his sleep – but
now he's waking up! In a minute he'll come out of his cave to
fight you!'

At this, Paul-Paul scrambled quickly to his feet and climbed
on to the unicorn's back. The unicorn was certainly completely
tame now. He had remained kneeling while Paul-Paul climbed
on to him, and now he stood up with a smooth movement, and
looked round at Paul-Paul as if to say, 'Hold on tight!' Paul-Paul
gripped the unicorn's sides firmly with his knees, and held the
unicorn's mane tight with both hands. 'Gee up!' he said, and the
unicorn began to canter round the clearing, with a steady, graceful
step. 'Beautiful!' cried Paul-Paul. The wind was rushing through
his hair, and the unicorn's strong body was rippling with muscle
under him, and it was just as beautiful as he had always imagined
riding a unicorn would be. If only they could go on riding and
riding for ever! If only there wasn't a dragon!

Now the unicorn stood still in the middle of the clearing. 'Are
you ready to fight the dragon?' Paul-Paul asked, and the unicorn
nodded his head. He didn't seem at all afraid. His bright blue eyes
were filled with the light of battle, and he snorted, and pranced,
and pawed the ground impatiently, waiting for the dragon to
come.

From where Paul-Paul was sitting, high up on the unicorn's
back, he could see quite a long way through the trees. And now,
for the first time, he saw that there was a great cliff of grey rock
rising out of the undergrowth not far away. Its face was hung
with black ivy, and all round it the trees and bushes and bracken
were charred and dead. At the foot of the cliff there was the dark
opening of a cave, with a lot of bones lying on the ground
outside it.

As Paul-Paul watched, there was an ear-splitting roar from
inside the cave, and out of the opening belched a great tongue of
flame. The trees and bushes shrivelled and turned black and the
ground shook as if in an earthquake. And then, to Paul-Paul's
horror, he saw a foot emerge from the cave – a huge, black,

webbed, misshapen foot with great curved claws! Then he saw
a second foot emerge, followed by a huge, black, hideous, grinning face, with hundreds and hundreds of sharp teeth glinting as
it grinned, and black smoke pouring from its nostrils!

The dragon looked round, and saw Paul-Paul and the unicorn.
'Ah-hah!' he roared. 'So you thought you were going to steal my
unicorn from me, did you, little boy? But I shall kill you, and eat
you for my supper!'

And with this the dragon crawled slowly out of his cave,
chuckling greedily to himself. Inch by inch, yard by yard, his
enormous, black, bloated body emerged, all covered with
armoured scales, with a long, black scaly tail with spikes in the end.
He opened his vast black wings, and flapped them, and grinned
triumphantly. Then he beckoned to the unicorn with one sharp
claw.

'Come here, my friend unicorn!' he said, in a friendly, sinuous
tone. 'Bring that tasty little boy to me!'

But the unicorn snorted, and pawed the ground, and pointed
his horn at the dragon.

'He won't come to you!' yelled Paul-Paul. 'I've broken your
spell, and he's going home to marry the princess!'

Just then, the dragon saw the bunch of passion-flowers in the

unicorn's mouth, and for a moment he cringed. Then he puffed himself up, and flapped his wings in hatred. 'Then I will kill you both!' he roared, and he came thundering through the undergrowth towards them, half galloping and half flying, and smashing all the trees and bushes in his path.

'Oh, help! Oh, help!' cried Paul-Paul in terror, as the dragon burst into the clearing. At once the whole clearing seemed filled with the flapping of webbed black wings, and the snatching of sharp claws, and the gnashing of grinning jaws. The dragon was so huge, he was all round them and above them at once, encircling them with his great scaly body and his long spiked tail, and blotting out the sky with his wings. His reared up head grinned down at them, ready to destroy them both with a single bite or a single belch of flame. There was no possible escape! The unicorn turned his head quickly this way and that, but there was no gap anywhere in the dragon's hard scales where the unicorn could stab him. They were doomed!

'Ah-hah-hah!' roared the dragon in cruel triumph, and he reared up even higher to swoop down and kill them. The whole sky went black, filled with his black wings and with the slimy, greenish underside of his body.

'It's the end,' thought Paul-Paul. And then he suddenly realized – there were no scales on the underside of the dragon's body! 'Quick! Stab!' he shrieked to the unicorn. 'It's our only chance!'

With one fierce toss of his head, the unicorn stabbed, ripping the dragon's belly open from end to end with his sharp white horn. The dragon gave a bellow of rage and pain, and crashed to the ground, while the unicorn and Paul-Paul leapt over his writhing coils to safety.

From the edge of the clearing, they watched the dragon die. He died slowly, flapping his wings and lashing his tail in agony. Smoke and flames still poured from his nostrils, while from his wounded belly oozed a horrible, stinking, boiling, bubbling green slime, which gradually burned a deep hole in the ground. Slowly the dragon began to sink down and down in the hole, screaming and writhing as he sank. Deeper and deeper grew the hole, darker and darker, and down and down sank the dragon. After a while he sank out of sight, and his screams sounded fainter and fainter from far below. And then at last there was nothing to be seen in the hole but a bottomless blackness, and nothing to be heard but silence.

'Tuwit-tuwoo! hooted the little white owl, rousing Paul-Paul and the unicorn, who were still gazing at the big black hole in the ground in a horrified trance. 'Back to the castle! The princess is waiting! Tuwit-tuwoo!' And he rose from the branch where he had been perching, and began to fly away through the trees.

Paul-Paul and the unicorn roused themselves, turned away, and then galloped after the owl. Faster and faster they galloped, with the ground rushing past beneath them, and the trees flashing past on either side. The unicorn was still carrying the bunch of passion-flowers in his mouth, and his blue eyes were deep and steady.

Paul-Paul was very happy. He loved the fast galloping, and he was longing to see the unicorn turn back into a prince again, when they crossed the drawbridge over the castle moat and saw the princess. But he was also very tired, and it was a long way back to the castle. So after a while he put his arms round the unicorn's neck, and rested his head against his soft, flowing mane, and closed his eyes. The rhythmic drumming of the unicorn's hoofs was very soothing, and soon the 'Tuwit-tuwoo! Tuwit-tuwoo!' of the little white owl flying ahead of them seemed to grow fainter and fainter, and to come from further and further away . . .

CHAPTER 15

Was it only a dream?

❧

'Tuwit-tuwoo! Tuwit-tuwoo!'

The little white owl sounded anxious all of a sudden. Without opening his eyes, for he was still very sleepy, Paul-Paul wondered why.

'Tuwit-tuwoo! Wake up, Paul-Paul!' the owl was hooting. 'You must wake up!'

'Oh, *must* I?' murmured Paul-Paul, still without opening his eyes. 'I'm *so* sleepy!' And he turned over to go back to sleep again.

Then suddenly Paul-Paul realized – he was lying on the ground! He had fallen off the unicorn's back! No wonder the owl sounded anxious!

'Oh, what's happened?' Paul-Paul cried, sitting up and rubbing his eyes. 'Has there been an accident? Did the dragon come back to life again? Has the unicorn dropped the passion-flowers, and run away again? Oh, what is it? – what's happened?'

Then he saw that the princess was kneeling beside him, smiling and stroking his hair. They were in a room in the castle.

'Oh, thank goodness! We've got back safely!' said Paul-Paul, closing his eyes again, and lying back in relief. 'Now we can all live happily ever after.'

'Paul-Paul! You've got to wake up!' said the princess, laughing. 'The museum's closing, and we've got to catch our train back to Fleury-des-Bois!'

At this, Paul-Paul woke right up with a start. It wasn't the princess kneeling beside him – it was Marie-Céleste! And they weren't in a room in the castle – they were in the secret room in the museum! Paul-Paul hadn't recognized it at first, because an electric light had been switched on, which made it look quite different. There was also a strange man in the room – but not the angry attendant, luckily. It was someone Paul-Paul had never seen before.

But Paul-Paul hadn't time to wonder who he was, or even to say hallo to Marie-Céleste. He scrambled to his feet. 'I must get back!' he shouted. 'I must get back to the forest at once! Something might have gone wrong!'

There, all round the room, was the dark green tapestry, striped with brown and silver trees, and spangled with passion-flowers. Paul-Paul ran quickly towards it.

But the strange man caught him before he reached it, and held him fast. 'Eh, eh, eh!' he said. 'Where do you think you're going?'

'Back into the tapestry!' cried Paul-Paul, struggling to get free. 'Let me go!'

But the strange man still held him fast. 'You can't go playing with tapestries here, you know!' he said. 'And especially not this one. It's very, very old and frayed. One good tug from you, and it would all fall to pieces! That's why we put "ENTRÉE INTERDITE" on the door. There's always a good reason for these things, you know!'

The man sounded quite kind, and Paul-Paul looked up at his face.

'Paul-Paul, this is the director of the museum,' said Marie-Céleste. 'He knows all about tapestries, and he's been so kind. I was terribly worried when I couldn't find you anywhere, and he helped me look for you. They'd already locked up this room for the night, but he unlocked it again, and here you were, fast asleep!'

'I *wasn't* asleep!' said Paul-Paul. 'At least, not all the time. I was in the tapestry, and I caught a unicorn, and killed a dreadful dragon!'

'Oh dear!' said Marie-Céleste, looking anxiously round at the tapestry. 'I hope you haven't done any damage.' And she added, to the museum director, 'He gets very carried away, sometimes, when he's day-dreaming.'

'I *wasn't* day-dreaming!' said Paul-Paul. 'It really did happen!'

But Marie-Céleste was taking no notice. She was listening to the director, who was saying, 'No, don't worry. I've already had a good look. He hasn't touched it at all.'

'Thank goodness for that!' said Marie-Céleste, with a sigh of relief. 'It must be a very precious tapestry.'

'Oh yes, indeed,' said the director. 'We believe it's one of the oldest tapestries in the whole world. But, of course, it's so faded and threadbare, no one can make out what it's about. Experts come from all over the world to see it, but no one has been able to discover what story it tells.'

'*I* know the story,' said Paul-Paul. 'All except for the very end, that is.' But no one took any notice of him.

'Some parts are in quite good condition still, of course,' the director was saying to Marie-Céleste. 'Here, for instance – ' and he showed her the part of the tapestry which Paul-Paul had looked at first, by the door. 'We assume that this part shows the beginning of the story. You can see a castle with a moat quite clearly here, in the middle of a forest. And these seem to be two horsemen riding out over the drawbridge, while this lady here is waving goodbye to them from a turret window.'

'That's the prince and the black baron going out hunting,' said Paul-Paul. 'And the lady is a princess.'

'Perhaps,' said the director, glancing down at Paul-Paul with an absent smile, as he led Marie-Céleste on to the next part of the tapestry. 'This part is rather faded,' he went on, 'but you can see that it's a turret room, with a lady sitting at a loom, looking very sad, and a white bird of some kind perched on the loom beside her. But goodness knows what it all means!'

'It's the princess and the owl waiting for the prince to come home,' explained Paul-Paul. 'But he couldn't, because the baron had turned him into a unicorn.'

'Hm, an interesting little theory,' said the director, glancing down at Paul-Paul with another smile.

'It isn't a theory!' said Paul-Paul indignantly. 'It's what really happened! I was *there*, and the princess told me.'

'What a vivid imagination!' said the director to Marie-Céleste with an amused raising of his eyebrows, and he led her on to the next part of the tapestry. 'Here, alas, the tapestry begins to become very faded and threadbare indeed,' he said, 'but one can just make out this small blue figure setting off from the castle on foot, accompanied by a lot of birds and animals.'

Paul-Paul knew who that small blue figure was, but he wasn't going to say, just so that the director could laugh at him. And then he looked down and saw that he was wearing his new brown suit with long trousers, and his best brown walking shoes again. He couldn't help feeling rather relieved to see that he hadn't lost those.

By this time, the director had led Marie-Céleste on to the next part of the tapestry, and when Paul-Paul looked at it, he gasped. For a long stretch, the tapestry was so frayed and faded that nothing could be made out at all, except for a few trees and bushes here and there, and even those were scorched and blackened. And in the middle of that long, faded, burnt stretch of tapestry, there was a big black hole!

'Most unfortunate, the director was saying, 'that this part should have been so badly damaged in a fire. It makes it quite impossible to understand the story.'

Paul-Paul said nothing. He was gazing in horrified fascination at that big black hole. Where was the dragon now? Had he climbed out of the hole again, and caught the unicorn?

Then suddenly Paul-Paul realized that the tapestry itself might tell him the end of the story. He ran quickly after Marie-Céleste and the director, who were already looking at the next part of the tapestry.

There, sure enough, were more threadbare trees, and the castle in the distance. And in the foreground of the tapestry there was a faint white shape, like a horse – but of course it wasn't a horse – galloping towards the castle, with a small blue figure riding on its back, and the little white owl flying ahead. They had reached within sight of the castle, at least. But it was the next picture Paul-Paul wanted to see – the one which would tell him if they had crossed the drawbridge, and the unicorn had turned into a prince again.

Paul-Paul ran on, eager to see the next and last picture – but there wasn't one. There was no more tapestry. There was only a torn, frayed edge, and then the door, leading out to the ordinary modern world.

'But where's the rest of the tapestry?' cried Paul-Paul desperately. 'There must be another picture! There must! There must!'

'Alas!' said the director. 'This is all we have of the tapestry. No one has ever found the rest of it.'

'But then how can we know how the story ends?' cried Paul-Paul. He was nearly in tears. He had been through all those dangers to save the prince and bring him safely home to the princess – and all for nothing, for now he would never know if he had ever arrived.

'Never mind, Paul-Paul,' said Marie-Céleste. 'We'll make up an ending on the way home. A really good ending! But now we must go, or we'll miss our train.'

'Oh, can't I stay just another minute?' pleaded Paul-Paul. If he could only get back into the tapestry for one moment, to find out how the story ended!

'We'll come back another day, I promise!' said Marie-Céleste, laughing. 'But now we *must* catch our train!'

'And I must lock up the museum too,' said the director.

Paul-Paul followed them sadly from the secret room. Now he would never know!

On the way home in the train, Paul-Paul told Marie-Céleste all about his adventure in the tapestry.

'Oh, Paul-Paul! What a lovely story!' said Marie-Céleste, when he had finished. 'I do understand now how important it was to know how it ended. But never mind! From what you've told me, it was sure to have ended happily. After all, the castle was already in sight, and the unicorn was still carrying the passion-flowers when you last looked, wasn't he? I don't see what could have gone wrong.'

But Paul-Paul still felt very sad. 'I wanted to see it happen!' he cried. 'I wanted to see the unicorn turn back into the prince, and

live happily with the princess ever after. Oh, if only I hadn't
fallen asleep!'

'It was only a dream, Paul-Paul,' said Marie-Céleste. 'Don't
upset yourself so. I think we tried to do too much today, and
you're very tired. Why don't you lie back and close your eyes, and
I'll make up a happy ending to the story for you?'

'It *wasn't* a dream!' cried Paul-Paul. 'It really happened, and
I don't *want* to be told stories. I only want to know the real
ending.' And with this, although he tried hard not to, he began
to cry.

'Oh, Paul-Paul, I do understand!' said Marie-Céleste, giving
him a hug. 'I do! I really do!'

After this, there seemed nothing more to say, and Paul-Paul
sat looking sadly out of the window. He wasn't quite sure himself
any more if it had been a dream or not, and this uncertainty made
him feel even sadder. If it had only been a dream, then he hadn't
met a unicorn after all.

By this time, Paris was already far behind them, and even the
Eiffel Tower had sunk below the horizon. The suburbs were
flashing past, and the country was beginning again. But Paul-Paul
leaned his head listlessly against the cold glass of the window,
taking no interest in what was passing. Soon the villages they
flashed through began to look more and more like Fleury-des-
Bois, and between them the setting sun was turning the cornfields
a beautiful gold. But somehow the beauty of it only made Paul-
Paul feel sadder than ever. Even when the dark line of the forest
appeared on the horizon ahead, and drew closer and closer until
the train was running along beside it, he still sat leaning his head
wanly against the window, feeling nothing at all.

Finally the train swung round the great curve in the line just
before Fleury-des-Bois, and he could see the village at the edge of
the forest ahead. The last rays of the sun were catching the church
tower as it rose above the tree-tops, and he could see the pigeons
circling round it, the sun catching their wings and making them
look like tiny flecks of light.

'The angelus is ringing,' he said, without much enthusiasm.

'It can't be,' said Marie-Céleste, looking at her watch. 'It's too late for that. And it's too early for evening Mass. You must be hearing things, Paul-Paul!'

The train was going very slowly now as it approached the station. The pigeons were still circling round the church tower, so Paul-Paul opened the window. The sound of distant church bells came clearly to them on the evening air.

'You're right! How very odd!' said Marie-Céleste. 'I wonder why they're ringing now.' And then she added, with a worried frown, as the bells went on ringing and ringing, much longer than usual, 'I do hope it doesn't mean bad news.'

Paul-Paul knew that sometimes church bells were rung for a long time when war was declared, or a house was on fire, or there was some other dramatic event. He stood up and leaned out of the window as the train pulled in to the station, hoping to see what might have happened. Marie-Céleste came and looked out too, over his shoulder.

An extraordinary sight met their eyes. A great crowd was standing on the station platform. Monsieur le Maire and Monsieur l'Abbé were there in the middle, and so were Marie-Céleste's parents, and Monsieur and Madame Dupré. Paul-Paul could see all his own family too, and just about everyone else he knew in Fleury-des-Bois. Even Mademoiselle Augustine and Mademoiselle Ernestine were there. And they were all smiling and waving, and all wearing their best clothes. The village band was there too, lined up in rows on the platform in their crimson and gold uniforms. As the train pulled in, they struck up the Wedding March, and several people threw their hats into the air and cheered.

'What on earth's going on?' said Marie-Céleste, laughing. And then suddenly she turned as white as a sheet, and sat down, closing her eyes.

In another moment, Paul-Paul saw why. For there, in the middle of the platform, between Monsieur le Maire and Monsieur l'Abbé, stood Jean-Pierre. He was wearing his best suit, with a black tie and a black arm-band on his sleeve, which meant that someone he knew had just died. Paul-Paul couldn't help hoping that it was Alphonse. But there wasn't time to think about that. Paul-Paul had noticed something much more important.

'Marie-Céleste! Marie-Céleste!' he cried. 'I know the end of the story now, and it *wasn't* a dream! And Jean-Pierre really has chosen us, and come back for ever!'

For Paul-Paul had seen that Jean-Pierre's bright blue eyes were deep, and steady and thoughtful; and in his hand there was a bunch of passion-flowers.